ALEXANDER

THE MCCLAINS BOOK 1

KIRSTEN OSBOURNE

UNLIMITED DREAMS

CHAPTER ONE

Madelina picked the child up in her arms and ran toward the castle where she lived with her parents and her aunts and uncles. Even with her vast knowledge of healing, she could not save the sick babe. Only one person could do that—her mother. She knew the knight was behind her as she ran, but she barely acknowledged him. What difference did it make if he discovered her family secret if a child's life was lost? She would save the child every day, and so would her mother!

When she reached the great hall, she called out at the top of her lungs, "Mother! This child is dying!"

She did not see her mother, only her aunt Christiana, but she knew that was good enough. Christiana would use her mind to communicate with her sister as she always did.

Christiana closed her eyes. When she opened them, she nodded at Madelina. "She is coming."

"Thank you, Auntie." Madelina sat down, cradling the

child against her, wishing she could call up power from within her to save the child as her mother could.

The man who had brought the child to the castle stared at her. "I was told you had a way with herbs and potions." He obviously could not understand why she was calling for someone else to save the child.

Madelina, still out of breath from her run, looked at the man before responding. "I do have a way with herbs, but everything I know is from my mother. She has a healing way about her." Many had called her mother a witch, but Madelina knew better. Her mother—and her two sisters— had each received powers at birth that they used only for good. How could anyone call that witchcraft?

Madelina herself had the power to call and calm storms, but she had apprenticed under the best medicine woman in the area. She wanted to be able to heal like her mother. As soon as she thought of her mother, she saw the older woman running toward her, her dress a blur of blue. Before Madelina could say a word, her mother was on her knees before her—hands outstretched to heal the child.

It only took a moment before the babe's fever was gone, and eyes were clear. They had been bloodshot with the fever, and the babe had been unable to make a sound. Madelina let out a breath. "Thank you, Mother."

The man looked at Madelina and walked toward her, reaching out to touch the child. "The fever is gone. She was burning up just a moment ago." He frowned in confusion. What was happening in this place?

Madelina frowned at the stranger. He must not be from the area because everyone around knew that her mother, Marina, had the power to heal with a touch. "Who are you?"

The man frowned at her. "My name is Alexander. I was sent with a message for Baron Roland from my father, Baron

Ralph. They fought with King William together, may he rest in peace."

"Roland is my uncle. I will take the message." Madelina held her hand out for the message with the gracefulness of a woman who had known power her entire life.

"But the child . . ."

"What about the child? She is fine now. Is she yours?" Madelina had a hard time believing the child could be his because she was dressed in peasant's clothes and he was obviously a nobleman.

"I found her lying along the path on the way here. I was surprised to find a child alone, but when I stopped to pick her up, she was burning with fever. A peasant I passed told me to bring her to Lady Madelina, who was skilled with herbs and potions, to heal her, so I brought her to you." He frowned. "How did your mother heal her?"

Mother raised an eyebrow. "I healed her with my touch, of course. There was no other way to save her life." She met the stranger's eyes. "I am Marina, wife of Charles, Roland's brother. I will take the missive to Roland."

Alexander bowed his head. "Thank you, Lady Marina."

Madelina was not surprised when her aunt took the message from her mother. "I will take it to my husband. I am Christiana, wife of Roland." Though both women were older, they held their heads high and proud. They were ladies by birth and by marriage.

"Thank you." Alexander watched as the two older women left the hall together, and he looked again at the young woman holding the child. "The babe is all right?"

Madelina nodded. "She is fine." She had no idea if the child was a girl, but she seemed like a girl to her, so she called her she. "We need to find her parents? She must belong to someone."

"I saw a burned hut a short distance from the road. I presume the parents had fever and their bodies were burned. I do not know why the child was spared."

"How far from here did that happen? If it was close, then people will come here to look for her. All of the people in the area know my mother and I heal anyone brought to us." She hugged ahpthe child tightly against her, hoping that no one would come. A child to raise would give her a true purpose in life—more than just apprenticing under her mother.

"And if no one comes for her?"

Madelina shrugged. "We will keep her and raise her as a member of our family."

"You would really do that? It is a *peasant* child."

"It makes no difference to us. People are people whether nobleman or peasants." She glanced up as her uncle entered the hall with her mother and both aunts at his side. Her aunt Eva must have been called to join them for whatever reason. Madelina did not like that this man knew the secrets her family held, but she could do nothing about it.

Roland stopped a foot in front of the stranger, his eyes traveling up and down the man. "You are the seventh son of my friend, Ralph? I have not seen him in many years."

"I am." Alexander was the seventh son of a seventh son as far back as their family knew, and that was back to their Viking ancestors. "My father asked me to greet you for him."

Roland read the scroll in his hand again before his eyes met Alexander's. "Your father has asked for an alliance through marriage. He said that as his seventh son, you have a great deal of luck. What does that mean?" Roland's eyes were narrowed shrewdly. He was a man of great power and influence, and no one in his presence forgot it.

Alexander shrugged. He had not realized his father was asking for a marriage for him, but he was not terribly surprised. He was already twenty-four summers, and he had never even courted a lady. His father wanted to see him married, and his luck would have pointed him to the right lady for his son. "It means that I am able to determine which fork to take in a path. I can guess which man is the one to be trusted. Little things like that. It comes from being the seventh son in a long line of seventh sons."

Roland would have once dismissed what the younger man was saying, but after years of being married to a woman who could communicate through his mind, he was inclined to believe such things were possible. "What is your hope for the future as a seventh son?"

Alexander took a deep breath. "I am not sure if you are aware, but my family has always provided for the seventh son first. I will inherit the castle where I was raised. My brothers have all married and moved on."

Roland raised an eyebrow at that. "I *was not* aware. Most families do things differently. Very interesting." He studied Alexander for another moment. "My four daughters have all married. And my sons have married as well. There is only one unmarried female left in the family."

Madelina blushed as she felt the eyes of everyone in the room on her. She knew her family despaired of her ever marrying. She was twenty summers old, and her father had suggested taking her to court many times, but her moods were too unpredictable. If she became sad, it could rain indoors, as it had many times in their castle. If she was angry, it could cause a tornado. She saw some snow start to fall from the ceiling, which her family would know meant she was embarrassed.

Alexander looked at the beautiful young lady, still holding the peasant baby against her breast. "Would you consider me as a possible husband?" He brushed a drop of moisture from his cheek, only then realizing it was snow. *But how? It is the middle of summer, and it is snowing indoors?* He looked around at the others in the room and realized none of them were surprised. Even the baby was perfectly content. "May I ask where the snow comes from?"

Madelina straightened her shoulders. If he was to consider her for a mate, then he must know of her affliction. "From me." All of the other females in her family had inherited powers that could help people. Hers were mere inconveniences.

"You?" He stared at her with surprise. First her mother had healed the babe with her touch, and now she claimed she was making it snow indoors. "How?"

She shrugged. "In my family, most of the women are born with special powers. We know not from whence they came, but we all have them."

Alexander looked at Roland. "This is true?"

Roland nodded. "My wife has the ability to talk to you in your head."

As soon as Roland finished speaking, Alexander heard the word "hello" in his mind. He stared at Lady Christiana in shock. "Did you do that?"

Christiana nodded, a smile lighting her face. "Hello, Alexander."

Madelina hid a giggle as her Aunt Eva stepped forward, a purple dragon swooping down from the ceiling and landing on her shoulder. "I am Eva. I have the power to make people see things that are not truly there."

Alexander swallowed hard, nodding. He had thought his family was odd with the luck the seventh son had, but this was truly amazing. He wondered how many people knew about this. "And you," he said nodding at Madelina's mother, "have the healing touch."

Marina nodded. "That I do."

He frowned at Madelina. "And what exactly is your power?"

Madelina had always thought of her power as more of a curse, which was why she had worked so hard to learn to heal people as her mother did. It also provided a cloak for her mother's powers when necessary. "I control the weather with my emotions."

He blinked a few times. "So, if we marry, I can expect a life of getting snowed on?"

She smiled wryly. "It only snows when I am embarrassed. If I am happy, the sun will shine. Different emotions cause different weather." She watched him carefully, wondering if he would run at the idea of her being so different than most women.

Roland spoke, commanding everyone's attention. "There will be no marriage until we have time to get to know you. You have yet to meet my brother, Charles, Madelina's father. I will not give you her hand in his stead."

"But . . ." Alexander took a deep breath. "I understand, sir. Mayhap I can stay nearby while you make your decision?"

Roland shook his head. "Nay, you will stay here. We will see you at all times of day and truly take your measure. Madelina is a precious gem, and she will not be allowed to marry a man who will not treat her as such." He turned to Christiana. "We will feast tonight to welcome a suitor for Madelina's hand."

Christiana nodded. "Aye, husband. I will go inform the kitchen." She rushed out of the hall, toward the back of the castle.

"And where may I put my things?" Alexander had not brought much with him. Just two changes of clothes. He would happily sleep on the floor if they so desired. Madelina was a beautiful woman, and he could not wait to spend time with her to get to know her better. She was obviously very

7

loved by her family, so he would have to make sure they were impressed by him.

Roland looked at Madelina. "Give the babe to your mother and show him to the blue room in the west wing. It will put him as far from you as possible and still have him in a comfortable room in my home."

Madelina did not think of disobeying. She may have powers that her uncle did not, but his orders were not to be thwarted. "I have not discovered her name yet, Mama." She pressed a kiss to the small cheek before turning her attention to their guest. "Do you want to get your things? We can have the stable lad tend to your mount."

"Yes, please." He watched her, thinking about what his father had proposed. She was a beautiful young lady, and she would suit him well . . . if looks were to be the only thing considered. But there was so much more.

He had no idea if she had a dowry, but it did not matter. His family was not lacking in land or wealth due to their luck. He had no idea if she would have the ability to run a large household, but that was just what she would need to be able to do as his wife.

As she led him to the stable, he took his horse's reins and followed, watching the gentle sway of her hips. His body reacted to her nearness, and he knew that her comely form would please him greatly. He hoped it would not take long for a marriage to take place.

"Milord, this is Gerald, our stable lad. Gerald, would you take Lord Alexander's horse and be certain to feed and water him?" Madelina asked.

Gerald bowed his head slightly. "Aye, milady. He is a fine horse." He patted the horse's muzzle and took his reins while Alexander got his things from a bag tied to the saddle.

"Thank you, Gerald," Alexander said, startling Madelina.

"Do you often thank servants for doing their jobs?" she

asked. Never before had she seen a member of the nobility outside her own family do so.

"Yes, of course. Whether it is their job or not, it is kind of them to help me. I try to never fail to show my appreciation." Alexander watched her. "Do you not approve?"

"Oh, I most definitely approve, milord. My family has always done the same, but I have never seen it from another. I believe it will afford you more of a chance to marry me." She walked back toward the castle, expecting him to follow.

"Wait, please."

Madelina turned to him. "Yes?"

"Since we are considering the idea of marriage to one another, would you consider calling me Alexander? Or even Alex, as my family calls me?"

She nodded. "Aye, Alex. And please call me Lina, as my family calls me." Not all her family called her Lina, but her siblings and cousins did, and she preferred the shortened version of her name.

"Lina? I had thought you would be called by your full name." He wanted to take her hand in his, but he was not sure how she would feel about it, so he walked beside her, not touching her except the occasional brush of his arm against hers.

"Often, I am called by my entire name, but all of my siblings and my cousins called me Lina."

"You are the last unmarried cousin?" he asked, curious about her family, which seemed to be very close.

"Yes, I am. I am a full six years younger than the closest cousin in age, so it is not surprising that I am the last to marry." She did not mention her affliction because he already knew about that. She did not need to pound it into his head with a mallet.

"And all the females in your family have powers such as

you do?" he asked, surprised that word of their family had not spread across all of England.

"Aye. One of my sisters is able to communicate with animals. One is able to change her appearance at will, making herself lovelier than she actually is. The strongest powers belong to my mother and two aunts. They had to fight a man who was attempting to conquer the world and win, or there would have been much hardship for many generations."

"That is fascinating." They had reached the castle, and she turned toward the staircase leading off to the left, while he followed.

"My uncle has said you will stay in the west wing in the blue room. It is his favorite room for guests to stay in—very comfortable but away from the ladies of the house."

He laughed. "He is a wise man." With that one sentence, she had explained how careful her uncle was with her virtue. He could not help but respect the man for the care he had taken with the woman he wanted to marry more and more as the afternoon wore on.

"Yes, he is. Wiser than you can imagine, I am afraid." She stopped at a door at the top of the stairs and opened it wide. "If you would care for a bath, I will have the servants prepare one for you. Or if you would like, I can give you a tour of the land and castle." She was not sure what made her offer the tour. It was not something she had ever done, but the man was a bit intriguing to her. Other men had come to ask for her hand, but she had denied them all. She wanted someone to desire her for herself and not for her familial connections.

"I would greatly enjoy a tour." Alexander walked into the bedchamber and put his things onto the bed. "Shall we go?"

Madelina smiled, nodding. "There is no need to show you this wing of the castle. It is only used for guests at this time. When the entire family lived here, it was occupied, but there is no need any longer. We all stay in the east wing near one another."

"I see." He followed her as she descended the stairs, one hand lifting the hem of her gown gracefully. She was not dressed in clothes that would have been acceptable at court, but she was pleasing to him. Her long green dress was made of simple cotton, allowing her ease of movement for her tasks. She was obviously not an idle woman. Her hands were calloused and rough, as if she did hard physical work at times.

As they reached the bottom of the stairs, she stopped. "Father, have you heard we have a guest?" She waved to Alexander. "This is Alexander. His father fought with you at Hastings. Alex, this is my father, Charles."

Charles tilted his head to one side, studying Alex. "Are you Ralph's son, perchance? You look quite like him."

Alex nodded. "I am. He sent me here."

"Roland told me an old friend had sent his son but not which old friend. I see that Madelina is showing you around." Charles offered his hand to shake. "It is good to meet you, and I will enjoy getting to know you."

"It is good to meet you, sir." Alex found he was nervous meeting the man who would decide whether or not he was allowed to marry Madelina. All of a sudden, it felt as if it had been his idea to marry the maiden, and he did not want anything to get in his way. His luck was proving true once again.

Charles looked back and forth between the two of them. "Enjoy yourselves."

She did not take them upstairs, and she did not show him the kitchens, but she led him to the four sitting areas that were on the main floor of the castle as well as the great hall, where they had feasts and ate supper on a regular basis. "Would you care to see the grounds?"

Alex shrugged. "I have been traveling for three days, and I am a bit weary. Would you mind if we sat down and just talked for a bit?"

"I am so sorry. You should have said something sooner. I would have been happy to sit with you." She led him to the closest sitting room and sat down on a window seat, tucking her legs under her. She knew it was not a ladylike way to sit, but if he was going to get to know her, then he should know the real her and not just what she projected to strangers.

He sat in a chair perpendicular to her, not at all disappointed that she made herself comfortable in his presence. "What do you like to do?" he asked.

She shrugged. "When I was little, my siblings and cousins and I would play together a great deal. Now I spend my spare time learning from my mother. Her healing abilities fascinate me."

"Do you sometimes wish you had her power instead of your own?" he asked. He could not imagine having any power and wishing for another, but he could see it was possible in this woman.

She smiled at how astute he was. "Most definitely. I can make it snow indoors or rain when I am sad, but what use are such things? A power like healing is something that can do good for others."

"I can see times when your ability to control the weather would come in handy." How could she not see the benefits of controlling weather?

She frowned at him. "Such as?"

Alex smiled at her. "Imagine we are in our own castle, the one I will inherit as soon as I marry, and there are invaders coming. We could find out about them many hours before they arrive. A tornado or a strong thunderstorm or even a blizzard would stop them in their tracks."

"Why did I never think of that?" Madelina asked. Her

father had never even suggested her helping them in a battle. She could see where it would be very useful, though.

"Because you are a gentle lady more interested in healing than in war, I would wager. And remember, I am surrounded by luck."

She smiled, delighted by this man and his company. Mayhap it was time she married after all.

CHAPTER TWO

Madelina spent the rest of the day with Alexander, chatting with him. She was careful to leave the door open, and quite often one of her aunts or her mother would stick their head in the room to check on them.

After several hours, her mother came into the room and sat down on the window seat beside her. "Supper will be served in an hour or so. Would you like to dress for the meal?"

Madelina had not thought of that. They were usually casual for meals, but with a suitor there for her, she would be expected to be more formal. "Yes, Mother." She stood, smiling at Alex. "Can you find your way back to your room? Or should I send someone with you?"

"I can make my own way." He stood and bowed his head. "I will see you at supper."

As soon as he was gone, her mother caught her hand and pulled her back down. "What do you think of him? I have never seen you spend so many hours with someone outside the family."

"Oh, Mama, he is a kind, gentle man. He said 'thank you' to Gerald for stabling his horse." Madelina knew her mother would understand the import of her words. She knew their family was different from others.

Marina smiled. "I think that is a very good sign indeed. Do you feel . . . attraction for him?"

Madelina blushed. "I feel like I would like for him to take my hand or kiss me. Is that attraction?"

"Very much so. I am pleased for you, daughter. I will have your father hurry as he finds out all he can about his family and past."

"Must he do that? It feels like we do not trust him . . ."

"I only have one youngest daughter and one last unmarried daughter. I do not trust anyone when it comes to my precious child." Marina got to her feet. "We must dress for supper. Wear your green velvet."

Madelina made a face. "But It is so hot. I will have to constantly make a wind blow through the great hall to avoid sweating."

"So? I see nothing wrong with that."

"Mama, where is the child?" Madelina felt that she had done something wrong not keeping the little girl within her sight. She had all but forgotten her as she had spent the day with Alexander.

"She is sleeping on a pallet in your room. One of the servants is with her. I judge her age to be around three. She hasn't spoken yet, but hopefully she will be able to give us her name." Her mother tilted her head to one side, considering. "You want to keep her, do you not?"

"If she has no other family, then yes, of course I do."

"It would not be easy to start out a marriage raising a child that is not even yours."

Madelina shrugged. "Honestly, Mama, if he does not feel

the way I do about raising a peasant child with no family, then he is not the man I want to spend my life with."

Her mother shook her head, a slight smile at her lips. "We may have raised you with just a little too much independence. You do realize that the final decision about whether or not you marry him will be made by your father and your uncle Roland."

"Well, of course. But they will take my opinion on the matter into consideration because they love me. I am valuable in their eyes."

"I hope you realize just how fortunate you are to have people who watch over you like you do."

"There is no doubt in my mind." Madelina sighed. "Now I will go and lace myself into my velvet dress and practice cooling winds." She hurried from the room, glad no one was watching her. She needed to learn to act a bit more ladylike eventually, but that day was not going to be the one where she accomplished it.

An hour later, she descended the stairs in her velvet gown, which weighed heavily on her. She was too hot, and she felt stifled in the thing, but her mother was right. It showed off all her assets beautifully.

When she reached the bottom of the stairs, she found Alexander waiting for her. He offered her his arm, and they walked to the table together. Her aunt had them sit beside one another, sharing a trencher. It was obvious she was in favor of a union between them, and from the look on her uncle Roland's face, he believed they were a good match as well.

Through the very long meal, her uncle questioned him about his family. "How much land did your father receive from King William for his service?"

Alex answered everything to her uncle's satisfaction, and

her father just seemed to watch Alex, as if he was trying to take his measure.

Madelina understood it was her duty to sit quietly and let her elders question him, but it was very hard for her not to speak her mind. Finally, she questioned her aunt in her mind. "What do you think of him, Aunt Christiana? Does Uncle Roland like him?"

Her aunt's lips quivered with amusement at the question. "I think he is going to make you a good mate, Madelina. Your uncle is very impressed with him, and he was fond of his father when they fought together. I believe the only things that could halt a marriage at this point would be if the two of you realized you did not get along well."

"I do not think that is going to happen."

Christiana gave a slight nod to her head. "I do not think so either. I hope he makes you as happy as you think he will."

Alex continued answering questions, unaware that there was a mental conversation concerning him occurring right there in front of him.

Madelina sat quietly, but she could not handle the heat for another moment. She closed her eyes and caused a cool breeze to blow through the great hall, smiling sweetly when her mother looked at her suspiciously.

Uncle Roland turned to her. "If you could make the breeze just a bit stronger and cooler, I would appreciate it."

Madelina bit her lip as she complied. "Is that better, Uncle?"

"Much."

Alex turned to her with a smile. "I wondered if that was you causing the breeze. It was wonderful."

"I am always happy to oblige." She took a bite of the meat from their shared trencher, a bit embarrassed, but very happy that he did not think something was wrong with her use of her powers.

After the meal, Alex asked her father formally, "May I take Madelina for a walk around the grounds, Sir Charles?"

Her father looked back and forth between the two of them, finally nodding. "Yes, but not too long."

As they stepped outside, Alex looked at her. "Your father does not trust me."

Madelina shrugged. "He does not *distrust* you. He just does not know you, and you are wanting to be alone with his youngest daughter. I have been coddled by sisters and brothers and cousins and aunts and uncles my entire life. It is part of being the youngest in such a large family."

"Your uncle Hugh . . . is he a Norman?" Alex asked.

Madelina was unsurprised by the question. Her uncle had neither the height nor the fair looks of a Norman. "No, he is not. He was born a peasant, but he saved Uncle Roland's life when he was but a boy and Uncle Roland could barely walk. After that he was raised with Roland as a member of his family, more to protect Roland than anything else. He married my aunt Eva, and the two of them have been very happy."

"Does it bother you that he was a peasant at birth?"

She shook her head. "Why would it? He is my uncle, and he loves me. Does it bother you?"

"Not at all. I believe that all men are equal but that some of us were privileged to be born into wealthy families. I know it is not the way most believe, but I do not really care if my opinions are popular."

She smiled at that. "My family feels the same. Uncle Hugh did not feel as if he was good enough to marry Aunt Eva from what I understand. She changed his mind, though."

Alex grinned. "I am glad to hear it. No one should be married to someone who thinks less of them." They had circled the castle twice, but he had not dared to go on the other side of the moat, where her family may not want her to be. He stopped under one of the windows, where they could not be seen, and took her hands in his. "I believe it was my luck coming into play when I was sent here to meet you, Lina."

She smiled. "I like that thought. I am glad you are here."

"Would you mind . . . that is . . . may I kiss you? I want to see if it would be as wonderful as I imagine it would."

Madelina stared up at him by the light of the moon. "I wonder the same things."

"So, may I?"

"Yes." She raised her lips for his kiss, having seen many kisses in her life. Her family was demonstrative with their feelings.

Alex took a step closer to her, his hands going to her tiny waist. "This dress must be very hot."

"Yes, but my mother said I needed to wear it, since it is my best." She shrugged. "The breeze in the great hall was the only thing that kept me going this evening."

He laughed. "I like that you were obedient to your mother, yet you still made certain you were as comfortable as you needed to be. You are a beautiful woman, Lina." Slowly, he lowered his lips to hers, finding hers pursed tightly together. His tongue stroked along her lips, and she opened her mouth a bit, enjoying the taste of him.

After a moment, he lifted his lips from hers, his forehead leaning against her own. "I want to marry you, Lina."

She smiled at that. "Give my father a few days to get used to the idea of losing me, and then ask for my hand."

"You will not refuse me?"

She shook her head, feeling the snow fall around them. "I will not refuse you." Her heart felt like it had just taken flight! Of course, she would not refuse him.

"Why does that embarrass you?" he asked, confused.

"Because marrying a man includes certain intimacies, and they came into my mind, and it embarrassed me, and then the snow started to fall . . ." She sighed. She really had no idea what the intimacies were, but she knew they had made her sisters blush. So, she was embarrassed. "It is not easy to spend your entire life with your emotions transparent to those around you."

"It will certainly shock my father when I bring you home and there are snowstorms in the castle. We will see how quickly he adapts to having you for a daughter."

"Do you have any sisters?" she asked.

He pulled her hand through his arm, and they resumed their walk around the castle. "No, I do not. The seventh son in my family never has daughters. Only seven sons. If you marry me, you will have granddaughters, but no daughters. Will that bother you?"

Madelina frowned until she remembered the peasant girl, sleeping on a pallet in her room. "It would, but I have a feeling the little girl you helped save today will have no family. I have already told my mother I plan to raise her as my own."

"What if I do not want her?" He did, but he wanted to know how she felt about the matter. And she needed to remember that if they were marrying, she would be making decisions for two, not one.

"I would be very disappointed in you, and I would think that perhaps I did not know you as I thought I did." Surely, he could see that they were the right choice for the child.

He smiled. "I do want her. I love the idea of her being a part of our family. I wonder how she will do with seven younger brothers."

"I have no idea, but I have a feeling we will find out. Unless Father finds out something terrible about you, of

21

course." She said it that way to see if he would tell her something terrible about him. If there was something that her father would object to, surely, he would tell her now.

"Am I being investigated?"

"Well, of course you are. My uncle sent out a messenger as soon as he told me to show you to your room. Do you really think he would not be careful about the man he allowed me to marry?"

Alexander smiled. "It seems like you are already used to being treated as a precious gem. I am glad because there will be no adjustment for you then."

She smiled at him. "Are you saying you will treat me as a delicate flower?"

He laughed. "I have this feeling you do not want to be treated like a delicate flower. Your hands are callused."

She shrugged. "I help Mother with a healing garden on the roof of the castle. We grow herbs for healing. If my mother gives people herbs and then boosts their healing a little bit when they come to see her, it keeps her secret intact. The peasants close to the castle know, of course, but most do not. That is how we like it."

"Do you enjoy helping her with the herbs and healing?"

"So much I could never express it. I feel like healing is a gift that should be passed down through the generations. If we are allowed to keep the peasant girl upstairs, she will be trained in healing, just as I was."

"Did your sisters train in healing as well?"

She shook her head. "No, they all just enjoyed their own powers. None of them were fascinated by the healing arts as I was. If only I could mix in a bit of my mother's magic and take it with us."

"Is your mother a witch?" he asked. He knew many would consider the question rude, but he hoped she understood that he meant it with an open heart. Being able to classify their powers would help him make decisions as they needed to be made.

"I would have to say no to that. We do not know where our powers come from, but we have to assume they came from God." She kicked up the wind a bit. The night was too balmy for her to be wearing such a heavy dress. It was July, and she was not a fan of being hot. "We all wear crosses, which we would not be able to do if our powers came from the evil one."

He nodded, thinking about her words. "Many have questioned the power that runs through my family as well. It is nothing like yours, but the luck that the seventh son receives is really quite remarkable at times."

"Give me an example."

"Well, I was in a burning house once, and I was trying to get some small children out. If I had stepped in one direction, I would have fallen through the floor to the cellar and my death. Instead I went the other way, and I was fine. I almost went the wrong way, but something inside me told me it was wrong."

"I see."

"And there was a business proposition made to me. A man was certain he was going to be able to earn a great deal of money off of a shipment coming into London. He wanted me to invest everything I had in this ship. A little voice in my head told me not to. I was sure it was a bad idea, and I tried to talk him out of it. The ship went down in the English Channel. He lost everything."

"So, if I marry you, I will never be a pauper. This is good to know." She smiled at him cheekily, knowing he would understand that she was joking. Somehow, she had found in him a man who understood her and whom she understood.

She had great feelings for him already. How had this happened?

"No, you should never be a pauper. I have never thought a great deal about my lucky ways, because they have always been a part of my life, but at this moment, I want to get down on my knees and kiss the ground, thanking God for the luck he has given me."

"And why is that?" Madelina asked, stopping with him just before they reached the entrance to the castle.

"Because it brought me to you, of course."

She laughed softly. "Why would you say that? What lucky thing brought you here? Was it not your father's message that brought you here?"

"Well, aye, but he could have sent any of my brothers over the years, and instead he chose *me* to come to your uncle." And looking upon her face, he knew he was the luckiest man in the world.

"There is that, I suppose."

He grasped her shoulders and pulled her to him, kissing her again, this time more passionately than the first. "I want our wedding to be soon, Lina. I am not sure how long I can wait to make you my wife."

Lina smiled up at him, amazed that this wonderful man had come here and felt the same for her as she felt for him. She said a silent prayer that her uncle's man moved quickly and did not run into any trouble. Even three days seemed too long to wait.

Late that night as she laid in bed, she thought of him and the way his lips had felt against her own. He was a good man. She could sense it, though it was not her power. Her aunt Christiana could usually sense evil intentions in a man, and she had felt nothing from him. No, she was sure they would be married quickly, and she would get to live happily ever after.

She heard a sound, and the little girl climbed into bed with her. "Mama?"

Madelina frowned. "Your mama is not here."

"She was sick."

"I know she was, but you were brought here to me so I could help you feel better."

"Mama died."

"Aye, I think she did. Do you have a grandmother? Aunts or uncles?"

"Papa died." The little girl was crying, and Madelina stroked her back, trying to soothe her.

"What is your name?"

"Letice. Mama calls me Lettie."

"Then I will call you Lettie. If no one comes here looking for you, then I will be your new mama, all right?" Madelina held the little girl, knowing that she was young enough that it would not be a terrible transition for her.

"Aye." With that one word and knowing she had be cared for, Letice closed her eyes and fell back to sleep. Madelina watched her sleep, wondering if she had just made a mistake. Alex had agreed to raising her if no one came for her, and she really hoped he had not just said it to appease her. She was keeping this girl. She loved her already.

———

ALEXANDER LAY IN HIS BED ACROSS THE CASTLE FROM HER, HIS hands folded behind his head. His incredible luck was really with him now. Madelina was the kind of gentlewoman he had spent his entire life dreaming he would find and marry. She was kind, considerate, and forward-thinking. And she could keep him cool during a heatwave.

He smiled as he thought of her powers. Most people would have scoffed, but he had seen them with his own eyes, and he was used to the idea of some families having a little something extra.

He prayed that her father would allow her to be his wife. Nothing else seemed to matter to him at that moment.

CHAPTER THREE

Madelina carried her new charge down the stairs to break the fast the following morning. She found her family all there already along with Alexander, who watched her with the child.

When she got to the table, she said, "This is Letice. She knows her mother and father died, and she is going to stay with us if no one comes for her."

Marina got up and took the child from her daughter. "How are you feeling this morning, Letice?"

"I am all better. I was sick, like my mama, but now I am not." Her blue eyes studied Marina intently. "You made me not sick anymore."

"I healed you, aye. I am so happy you are feeling better." Marina handed the girl back to her daughter, and Madelina set her on the bench between her and Alex. Marina then looked at her sisters. "I think we are going to be sewing for a few days, sisters. We need to make sure my new grand-daughter has clothing."

They had burned the girl's clothes shortly after healing her and borrowed a nightgown from one of the servant's

KIRSTEN OSBOURNE

children. "I will help with that, Mother," Madelina agreed readily. She was not about to leave the work to the other ladies.

"You will not. Your job at the moment is to get to know the young man sitting beside you," Roland said firmly.

Madelina was more embarrassed than ever when a gentle snowfall started in the hall. "Aye, Uncle."

Alexander laughed softly. "I like this way you show me your emotions."

"I do not." Madelina shook her head. "No one else has to deal with storms inside when they get embarrassed or sad."

"Will it rain inside?"

"It can. Of course, if there is a fire, I can put it out!" Madelina had listened to him the previous day, thinking about ways that her powers could actually help people and not just embarrass her.

"And there will never be a drought as long as you are around." Alex grinned at her, wishing he could kiss her good morning, but not with her entire family watching. "Would you care to walk with me after we finish our meal?"

She nodded. "Mayhap I can get my bow and arrows, and we can hunt!" She had learned to hunt from her mother and her aunts when she was young. Her father and uncles had never thought much of women hunting, but they had all approved of the idea of their daughters being able to defend themselves, so they had allowed the training.

"You can shoot a bow and arrow?" he asked, surprised. It was not something most ladies were capable of.

"Of course, I can." Madelina loved the look of astonishment on his face. She thought to her aunt Christiana, "Thank you for teaching me. It made this moment so special."

Christiana grinned. "Eva and your mother agree with me when I say, 'We are very proud of all of your skills. Not just

28

the ladylike ones.' We are not about to send our daughters out without skills to live in a man's world."

"Tell them thank you as well!" Madelina looked down at Letice. "I am going to go for a hunt this morning. Will you be happy with my mother and her sisters?"

Letice nodded. "Aye."

Charles frowned at Alexander. "I will allow you to take her hunting, but you must take four of our men with you. I keep my daughter safe."

Alexander nodded. "I expected nothing less, milord."

After their meal, Madelina hurried up the stairs to fetch her bow and arrows. When she returned with them slung over her shoulder, Alex could not help but smile. She was not the lady he had expected that he would someday marry—she was so much more.

They went to the stable with four of her father's men trailing behind them. Madelina turned to the men. "Keep us within sight but stay far enough back that our conversation is not overheard." She hated that they had to have someone following them about, but they would do it on her terms because that was how she did things.

He was surprised to see that she did not saddle her horse, but instead, she mounted it bareback. "Are you not forgetting something?" he asked, indicating the back of the mare.

She laughed. "I do not like saddles, and neither does my lady. We ride together much more happily without that burden. Follow me. I will show you the best hunting ground in the area!"

She led him over the lowered bridge and across a field. Watching her ride was a thing of beauty. She seemed to be one with her mare. He had never seen a lady ride with such pure delight on her face, and he knew it was her training. Her mother and aunts had obviously had more of a free reign with the girls in their household than most did.

He caught up, riding beside her. When she stopped her horse and dismounted, she laughed happily. "No one is ever willing to ride with me. I am not allowed to go out with just the knights, so I am often cooped up at home. I am glad you are here."

He caught her hand, and they went into the forest there. She squatted down, her arrow notched and ready. He frowned but stood silently, watching her. It did not take long before a rabbit hopped along, and she shot it with one arrow straight through the heart.

One after another, she shot eight rabbits, and strung them all together while he stood watching. "I know what we are having for supper this evening," she said, grinning at him. Her father's men had stayed just close enough to see them as she had instructed. "I wish I could kiss you this morning, but Father's men are not giving us a moment's peace."

"Later," he promised her, his eyes gleaming. "I look forward to the man your uncle sent coming back with word that I am safe."

"I am a little sad that I will have no daughters to pass my powers on to," she said softly.

"Mayhap my family's luck will mix with your family's powers, and something wonderful will happen." He did not really believe such a thing could happen, but who would have believed in a family of lucky men and a family of powerful women to begin with. God was capable of anything He chose to do.

"And mayhap we are being silly hoping for such a thing," she responded. "We should get these rabbits to Cook. She makes a rabbit stew that will make you cry with pleasure."

"I can think of a few other things that will make me cry with pleasure as well," he said with a wink. He was not even surprised when the snow started falling under the July sun.

"Come, let us go back to the castle. Mayhap we can find a quiet room for a while."

She knew he was thinking of kissing her again, and she was thinking of letting him. Despite her embarrassment, she loved his touch. She loved his words. She knew that it would not be long before she would love this man, who would hopefully be her husband.

When they arrived back at the castle, they took their mounts to the stable and left them with Gerald. "Thank you," she said to the young man.

He inclined his head with a grin. "Did ya surprise him with yer skills?"

"Of course, I did. No one thinks a lady can ride until they see it for themselves."

Gerald laughed softly, taking both the horses. He had worked for the family for a while, and he was always proud of the ladies' skills with the horses.

She had the rabbits strung together and thrown over her shoulder as they walked into the castle. Roland looked up and smiled. "Cook will make a wonderful stew with those. Take them straight to the kitchen. I am hungry already."

Alexander followed her into the kitchen, watching the way she interacted with the servants. "Cook! I brought you something!"

Cook, an older woman with no teeth left in her head, turned and smiled. "Wanting some of my rabbit stew, are ya?"

Madelina passed off the rabbits and leaned down to kiss the cook's cheek. "I always want some of your rabbit stew. You are a sorceress in the kitchen."

"And you are a sorceress out of the kitchen!" Cook said with a laugh.

"It is my lot in life," Madelina said as she headed for the door.

Alexander smiled at her. "Does everyone here in the castle know about your powers?"

She nodded. "Many of the servants were here when my father and uncles came to claim the manor my mother and her sisters were protecting."

"And they were able to defeat them?" he asked with surprise.

"Come, and I will take you to a sitting room and tell you the whole story." She had heard many times the story of the Battle of Hastings and the battle that had followed it when her uncle Roland came to claim the home, land, and bride he had been given.

As they passed through the great hall, her father called out to her, "It will be time to eat in less than an hour. Be sure your mother can find you!"

"If Mother cannot, Aunt Christiana always can!" she retorted. She had not been taught to be afraid of men. Instead she had been taught from her cradle that men and women were each powerful in their own ways. Her father had not especially liked that she had been taught that way, but as he had been off seeing to the defense of their new home, her mother and her aunts had gotten their way.

Alexander waited until they were in the sitting room before he pulled her into his arms and kissed her. "I have been waiting to do that all morning."

She smiled, her green eyes shining. "I happen to like it when you kiss me that way."

"Good, because I like it a lot, too." Alex led her over to the window seat, and this time they sat there together. She once again curled her legs underneath her, and she rested her head on his shoulder as she told the story of how the army had come and fought her mother, her two aunts, and some servants.

"So, they were actually able to turn the men back with the vision of an army?"

"Aye, but only for a short while. They came back all too soon, well before Aunt Eva was ready to cast the image of an even larger army. Uncle Roland says that when he saw the women on the parapet with their bows and arrows, he knew the army could not be real. No one with an army that size would allow their women to help in the fight. So, he aimed for Aunt Eva, and the army disappeared. Not before Aunt Christiana shot him, though!"

"Your aunt shot the man who had come to marry her?" Alex could not help his laughter. It came booming out, filling the room with his joy. "And he still married her?"

"The very next day. Mother healed him at Aunt Christiana's insistence, though. Mother wanted to leave him in pain. She is almost never in favor of not healing someone, but she had no desire to be a captive of the Norman army."

"It seems odd that your mother and aunts were Saxons, and I do not even know why. My mother was a Norman, and I was born after we came here to England."

"Where do you live?" she asked. "You are not in London, are you?" She hated the idea of anything to do with court. She was a country girl, and she would prefer to stay that way.

"No, we are up in the north. Just past York to be exact."

"But you do not live in the city? I could not imagine having to go to court. If I wore my velvet dress and I got too hot, I am not sure how all the lords and ladies there would feel about snow falling in the middle of the palace." Madelina knew she would not fit in with proper ladies.

"We are much more casual in the north. The biggest city we visit tends to be York and not often." He smiled at her. "We are far enough south that the Scots are not constantly raiding us, but we are far enough north that we are not expected at court on a regular basis."

"Oh, good. Sounds like the perfect place to be."

"I certainly think so." He eyed her skeptically. "How will you feel about leaving your family?"

"Aunt Christiana is able to keep tabs on family with her power. As long as I communicate with her often, and with my mother through her, I do not think there will be a problem. You will not mind if Mother and I write letters back and forth, will you?"

He should not have been surprised that she could read and write, and yet he was. It was not a skill most ladies had. "You read and write?"

She shrugged. "Mother taught us when we were young. She has had me write down recipe after recipe for medicines. That way when I am on my own, I will still be able to do the healing work that I am so fond of."

"You astonish me more and more by the minute, Lina. You are truly a special young lady."

The snow fell once again. "I am no different than the other ladies who were raised under this roof. It was the influence of my mother and aunts that made us all extraordinary." She looked down at her hands for a moment. "You are not intimidated by my strangeness?"

"Intimidated?" He shook his head. "Never. In awe? Aye. I admire you a great deal, Lina, and I am very excited to start our lives together."

"What if my father will not agree to our marriage?" She knew there was little likelihood of that, but she wanted to be prepared for the worst.

"I will sneak you away and marry you anyway," he said with a grin. "I do not think there will be a problem, though. My father was friends with your father at one time, remember. I believe It is just a matter of waiting for the man your uncle sent to come back, and we will be wed."

"I should start work on a wedding gown. Do you have a favorite color?"

"Green," he said, looking into her eyes. "I want to match your eyes. I cannot wait until we have children with eyes that are green."

"Do you think we will?" She looked at his eyes. "Your eyes are more of a grayish blue. Do you not think that the boys will have your eye color?"

He sighed. "You found me out. Every boy in my family for generations has had the gray-blue eyes. I was just dreaming of green eyes. Just for a moment."

"I happen to love the color of your eyes, so I do not think that is a bad thing."

He leaned down and kissed her once more, softly and tenderly.

A knock on the door had them jumping apart. They had left it partly open because she knew her family would accept nothing less. She turned to see her father standing at the door. "Madelina? I do not believe you were taught to behave that way."

She lowered her head, ashamed. Hail began to fall from the ceiling. Her father covered his head with his arms. "Make it stop!"

Madelina concentrated and made the hail stop falling, but she could see her father had a knot on his temple. "I am so sorry, Father!"

Charles sighed. "Go get your mother to heal it. I want to talk with your young man anyway."

Her eyes were wide as she looked from one man to the other. The two men she loved most in the world, and neither looked as if he was willing to give so much as an inch. "Aye, Father."

She stood up and hurried from the room, all but running to the great hall, where she knew she would find her mother.

"I made it hail, and Father has a lump on his forehead. Come quickly!"

"A lump on his forehead? He will not even let me heal something so paltry."

"He said to bring you!" Madelina grabbed her mother's hand, tugging her behind her.

When they reached the room where Madelina and Alex had been kissing, she saw her father and Alex standing toe to toe. "Do something, Mother!"

"What were you doing that you were ashamed enough it hailed, Madelina?"

"Father caught us kissing."

Marina wiped the smirk off her face. She could not count the number of times she and Charles had hidden to kiss before they married. Of course, her daughter would be just like her. "Let me see to your lump, husband."

Charles glared at her. "I need to finish my discussion with Alexander."

"No, I do not believe you do. I will heal you, and you can talk to him after the noon meal when your temper has healed."

"I said you will wait, wife!"

"And I refuse to wait. You sent our daughter to get me, so you must be in great pain." Marina stepped between the two angry men and raised her hands to heal her husband.

Madelina nodded to Alexander, and the two of them hurried off to the great hall. "What did Father say to you?"

"That I cannot dishonor you with such behavior. That I am not worthy of marriage to you." He shook his head. "You would think he had found us unclothed!"

"Alex!" she said, a bit shocked. "I am sorry he behaved that way, but I assure you, I have never behaved the way I have since you have arrived. He is not used to this sort of thing from me."

"That pleases me." He ran his hand through his thick red hair. "If I can convince your father of the need, would you marry me this day?"

She nodded, tears springing to her eyes. She knew they had been talking as if them marrying was a foregone conclusion, but to have him ask filled her with gladness. "Aye, I would."

"Then I will speak with him and your uncles over the noon meal. Surely your uncles will be able to talk some sense into your father. He knows that I have feelings for you, and delaying our wedding just makes things more difficult for both of us."

"I have not made a special gown for our nuptials, though."

"You do not need anything new. Wear the green velvet you wore last night. Wear what you have on!"

She looked down at herself and laughed. "I cannot marry in my hunting clothes!" She wore an old brown dress that had been mended many times over the years. She was certain it had belonged to at least two of her sisters before her and possibly a cousin as well.

"I do not know why not. You look beautiful in anything."

"I want to kiss you for saying something so sweet to me, but I am afraid my father would not be pleased." She smiled at him.

"Let us go to the great hall and explain our problem to your uncles before your father arrives. Mayhap they will join our side."

When they arrived in the great hall, Alexander went to her uncle Roland immediately. "I would like to marry your niece. I feel as if we have gotten to know one another well, and we should marry now."

"Gotten to know each other well in less than a full day?" Roland asked, raising an eyebrow. "What say you, Madelina?"

"I want to marry him. Father just caught us kissing in the

sitting room, and he is out of his mind with anger. Please help us convince him to let us marry." She knew avoiding the true issues would only make things harder. No, she needed her uncle to know the full story before he made his opinions known.

Roland looked between the two of them, frowning. "I suppose it is for the best." He shook his head. "My man is not back with his report on you yet, but I have made some local inquiries. Your reputation is impeccable."

Christiana smiled. "Your mother and aunt Eva and I spent all day yesterday sewing. There is a new blue velvet dress ready for your wedding."

Madelina flew into her aunt's arms, hugging her tightly. "Thank you!" She turned and hugged Eva as well. "I have the best aunts in all of England!"

Eva laughed softly. "That you do. Now all we have to do is convince your father."

Madelina sighed. "It does not sound like an insurmountable task until you say it that way." She worried her father would never let her marry Alex now that he had seen them kissing.

Hugh reached out and grasped her hand. "You will marry this man. He makes you happy."

Her uncle was a man of few words and had been for as long as she had known him. He was completely devoted to her uncle Roland and to his wife, Eva. "Aye, I will, Uncle Hugh." She squeezed his hand and smiled at him.

Her parents joined them in the great hall just minutes later. "You will stay away from my daughter!" Charles yelled at Alexander.

Roland shook his head at his brother. "No. It is time for a wedding. You know it as well as I do. They care for each other, and that is why they kissed. It is not an ugly thing."

Charles sat down heavily. "Are all of you against me on this?" he asked, looking around the table.

Marina answered him. "I am never against you, but this time I am very much *for* our daughter."

He sighed. "Well, if you disagree with me, then I know I am beaten." Looking at Madelina, he shrugged. "I guess you are marrying him." He did not look happy at the prospect. Resigned was a better description.

"Today?" she asked softly. It was what they both wanted, and she knew he was the only one who could possibly object.

Charles looked at his brother and their friend. Both of them nodded at him. "Today." He rubbed his hands over his face. "I am not ready for my last baby girl to marry."

Marina leaned into her husband. "You do not have a choice."

"I guess not." Charles sighed heavily. "We should discuss her dowry."

Alex shrugged. "I am not concerned with a dowry."

"I am!" Madelina insisted. "I will not come to you a pauper when my father set a dowry aside for me at my birth."

"We will talk about it after the meal," her father said, still seeming annoyed with the entire situation. "When will you marry?"

"Just before supper," Madelina said. "I want to marry in the courtyard while the sun is setting."

"You are going to be hot in the blue velvet dress we made you," her mother warned her.

"I will make a breeze. It amuses everyone anyway. Or mayhap I will make it snow . . ."

"You will not get us all wet at your wedding, Madelina!" her aunt Eva insisted.

"Aye, Aunt Eva. Since the sun is setting later, would you provide the visual I need?"

"What are you going to do without our powers to call on constantly?" Eva asked with a smile.

"I do not know. Hopefully I will not make it rain inside for missing all of you." Madelina smiled. "We will be living in his family's castle just north of York."

Marina bit her lip. "That is so far. We may never see each other again."

"I will write to you at least once every fortnight, and I will send you messages through Aunt Christiana."

Christiana frowned. "I am not sure I will be able to communicate from that far away, but I will do my best."

"I know you can do it, Auntie. Because you will have someone listening hard for any message you want to send."

Madelina looked over at Alex with a smile. They would be married before nightfall. She was actually going to marry him.

CHAPTER FOUR

Madelina was separated from Alexander for the rest of the day. She was bathed by her mother and her aunts, who talked to her of what would happen on her wedding night. The snow splashed into her bathwater.

"Do all three of you need to be here to discuss this with me?" she asked.

Marina grinned. "Of course, we do. We are triplets after all."

Madelina sighed. "I am going to miss all of you. I have not talked to Alex yet, but I am hoping I can talk him into staying for at least another day or two. I need time to say goodbye."

"You cannot force him to stay. It is his right to take you to his home. He will want to show you off to his parents and brothers." Marina washed her daughter's back for her. "I take it I will have seven grandsons from you."

Madelina nodded. "If what Alex tells me is true, and I have no reason to doubt him. At least I will have little Letice, too. I will be able to teach her the healing arts like you taught me."

"We will have to get your medicine jars ready," Marina said. "We are going to need at least a night, probably two, to get you completely ready to go. I want to have a few more clothes made for you as well."

"I am not sure how he will take to the idea of staying several more days, Mother."

Christiana shrugged. "We will get everything ready as quickly as we can. We made a couple of dresses for Letice this morning while you hunted and kissed."

"I am not ashamed of kissing him now that it led to my wedding coming earlier than it would have. I am ready to be his bride."

"You met him *yesterday*," Aunt Eva reminded her. "You do not know everything about him yet. Give him some time."

"Time for what?"

The three older women exchanged a look. "Give him time to adjust to you and learn your ways. Most men do not allow women to act as the girls in our family always have." Christiana frowned at her niece. "He is going to need *time* to learn our ways."

"You do not think he will try to change me, do you? Because he will not. He is told me he admires the way I do things."

"It is one thing to admire it in a girl as you get to know her and another to adjust to being married to that same headstrong woman. I fear we have spoiled you by making you feel like it is all right for you to ride bareback and hunt whenever you wish."

"You have not." Madelina was certain. They were worrying for nothing. She was going to marry a man who understood her as she already was.

After drying off, she put her shift on, and her mother brushed her hair dry. With as long as it was, the process took hours, and the women sat and told stories of their early marriages and the trouble they had gotten into with their husbands for their own headstrong ways.

When her hair was dry, her aunt Eva put it into an intricate knot atop her head. She stood looking at the three of them, feeling as if she were someone else, just observing the whole thing. "Thank you for raising me the way you did. Thank you for making me strong."

The three older women walked to her, and the four hugged together. "I am very proud of you, Madelina. You not only learned to use your gift, you learned to heal as well. You will be helping many people," her mother said softly.

"And having babies," Madelina said with a laugh. The idea of having seven sons was a little bit daunting.

"You just let your aunt know when you are expecting, and I will be sure to be there for the births of those babies," her mother told her. "Your father will love it if I have to go there to help with them, will not he?" She had already helped seven of her own grandchildren into the world. Seven more would make her happy and proud.

Madelina laughed. "I hope someday he comes to realize what a wonderful man Alexander is."

"Oh, I have no doubt he will!"

"I will check and see if they are ready for us," Christiana said, closing her eyes. What she did needed no explanation because the others had seen it so many times. "Roland says they are waiting for us."

Madelina opened the door to see her father waiting for her. The three older women hurried down the stairs to wait in the great hall, while Charles offered his arm to his daughter. "Thank you, Papa."

Charles shook his head. "I still do not like him."

"You do not have to live with him." Madelina smiled up at him, hoping he would see that she was right. She needed to be married to the man as much as her father needed to be married to her mother.

"I hope he accepts you for the precious jewel you are." They walked down the stairs arm-in-arm. When they got outside where Alexander stood with the priest, Charles leaned down and kissed her cheek. "Be happy, my daughter."

"I will, Papa!" She hugged him close before joining hands with Alexander.

Twenty minutes later, they were declared husband and wife, and they kissed once more. Her father was not even allowed to complain this time, though afterward, she could see on his face, he wanted to.

During the wedding feast, she sat nervously beside Alex. "May we stay here for a few days before we move on to our home?" she asked softly.

Alex frowned. "Why?" Her father had so much hostility toward him, it would be difficult to stay.

"My mother and I need to gather all the healing balms and potions we have made for me to use. She has knowledge of them, but she has taught me to use them. So, I will take them, and I can heal *our people* as they need it."

He sighed, nodding. "Aye, we can stay for two nights."

It would be barely enough time, but if they worked quickly, she and her mother and aunts could make it work. "Thank you." She quickly sent a message to her aunt Christiana. "We are staying two nights. Please let mother know that we must work quickly to get all we need to do finished."

"I will."

A moment later, her mother nodded at her, letting her know she had gotten the message.

Alex frowned at her. "Are you communicating with your aunt through thoughts?"

"Aye, I wanted to let my mother know that we would stay

another two nights. I told my aunt, so she could tell my mother. Is that a problem?"

"It is just strange to be left out of conversations in such a way. Your family does not consider it rude to talk through thoughts so not everyone can hear?" He was not angry, but he was glad she would not always be able to do it. He was ready to get her away from the house where she had grown up so they could start their lives together.

"I never really thought about it that way," Madelina responded. "It has just always been the easiest way for us to pass a message along."

"I see." He did, but then he did not. It was like keeping secrets and whispering to him, and both were quite rude in his opinion.

"I am sorry," she said softly. She was not sure that she would stop talking to her aunt the way she did because it was very efficient, but mayhap she would stop being quite so obvious about it. No reason to upset him.

Her uncle Hugh got out his lute and played and sang for them. The songs he sang were always in the language of the French, but that did not bother any of them since they were all fluent in the language. His voice was smooth and melodic, and they all enjoyed his singing a great deal.

Finally, Alexander got to his feet. "Thank you for the wedding feast. I think it is time my wife and I retire."

Her mother got to her feet. "I will prepare my daughter for bed." She walked to Madelina and linked arms with her, going up the stairs. "We should have thought to have your clothes for the morrow in his room tonight. It would not do for you to wear the same clothes."

"I did not even think of it."

"Well, I know Alex is very ready for your wedding night. I hope you are as well, daughter."

"Are you worried that I am not?" Madelina asked,

surprised. "I thought you and the aunts told me everything I needed to know."

"Aye, we did. I just hope you are ready for all the emotions that go with it. You will be tied to Alexander forever after tonight."

Twenty minutes later, Marina left her daughter in Alex's bed, completely naked as was the custom. "Just do as he says and try to please him," she said.

Madelina lay in the bed, very embarrassed. Her entire family would know what they were doing, and they were doing it under her family's roof. Certainly, this was not how marriages were meant to be. She should have told him she wanted to leave that very night, not stay another two nights. What had she been thinking?

Alex came into the room a short while later, a candle in his hand to light his way. He set the candle onto a low table and quickly stripped out of his clothes, very anxious to get on with his wedding night.

He slid into bed beside Madelina and pulled her to him. "I am not sure I can do this here," she whispered.

"What do you mean?" Alex was already frustrated by some of the events of the evening, especially the way her father acted as if he was attacking her. She could not be trying to refuse him a wedding night, could she?

"I . . . it feels wrong to consummate our marriage under my father's roof . . ."

He groaned, rolling to his back. "Are you serious?"

"I am sorry, Alex."

"Let us go outside then. We will go to the forest where we hunted today and make love there."

She shook her head. "It would not be safe." Surely, he could wait a day or two.

"Can I at least kiss you? Your father's seen me kiss you twice, so they know we were doing that."

"Aye, of course." She rolled onto her side, facing him. "I am not trying to upset you, Alex. It just feels wrong."

"I know. I understand." He did not, but what else should he say? She was his new wife, and he had no desire to upset her either.

He cupped her face in his hands, lowering his head to kiss her softly, slowly deepening the kiss. His hand moved under the sheet to stroke her breast, just the side of it with his knuckles. "You are so soft, Lina."

She wrapped her arms around him, holding him closer, one of her legs resting atop his. "I like how it feels when you touch me."

"I want to make love to you," he said softly, his hands cupping her breasts fully, stroking her soft skin.

"I want you, too. I do not want to wait."

"Then we should not. Your family will think we made love whether or not we do. Why not just make it true?"

His reasoning made sense to her. Finally, she whispered, "All right."

As soon as he had her permission, he rolled her to her back, his hand going between her thighs and stroking her there. "I do not want to hurt you."

She did not want to be hurt either. Her arms wrapped around him. "What should I do?"

"I have no idea," he said with a laugh. "I have never done this before either."

"You have not?"

"No. My father always said that part of me should be saved for the woman who would have my sons. So, I waited." He kissed her again, this time his tongue strongly invaded her mouth as his body wanted to invade hers. He moved over her, his body completely covering hers.

Always sensitive to heat, she made it snow there in the room, so they would not get too hot. He shivered. "Stop it!

47

Why are you making it snow?" Was she trying to make him stop with the cold?

"I am sorry. I was hot. I did not think you would mind."

"Mayhap a gentle cooling wind, but we do not need snow." He grinned down at his wife. Who else would make it snow on her wedding night?

He kissed her again, holding her face in his hands as he entered her in one quick stroke. As soon as he was buried deep within her, he raised his head, needing to know she was all right. "Lina?"

Her eyes were wide as she looked up at him, the only light in the room the small candle on the table. "Aye?"

"Am I hurting you?"

"Just a little. Mama said the pain would stop quickly." She stayed perfectly still, hoping it would stop soon. It felt like it had lasted forever already. "Are we finished?"

Apparently, her mother had not explained what would happen in great detail. "We have barely started, love."

"Oh." She could not imagine what else he could possibly do that he had not already done, and then he pulled out and moved back inside her. "Oh! That felt good."

"I am so glad!" He started moving more quickly, finding his pleasure within her and resting his head on her shoulder. "I am sorry," he said a long while later when his breathing had returned to normal.

"Why are you sorry?" she asked. "That was nice."

"I am sorry because you did not feel the same pleasure I did."

"I do not think a woman is supposed to feel that kind of pleasure." She turned to her side snuggling close to him. She was just relieved she had fulfilled her duty with him.

"You are, and you will," he promised. Not that she heard him because she was already asleep. He knew, though. He would make certain that the next time, she enjoyed it as much as he did.

———

WHEN SHE WOKE THE FOLLOWING MORNING, ALEXANDER WAS already gone from their room. She sat up in bed looking around for him, but he was not there. She pulled her clothes on, feeling tender between her thighs. She thought about asking her mother to heal her, but she knew she would be too embarrassed to explain why. Not that her mother would not understand.

When she got downstairs, everyone was eating, and little Letice looked sad. "Why are not you happy?" she asked, kissing the girl's cheek.

"I slept alone." Letice frowned at her.

"Oh, I see. Well, I am married now, so I cannot sleep with you every night." She did her best not to blush as she looked at Alex, but there were snowflakes drifting through the great hall.

Charles shook his head at her. "I love you, Madelina, but it will be nice not to have to deal with weather *inside* the castle constantly."

Madelina wrinkled her nose at him. "You love me for the weather in the hall."

"I am not sure that is the reason I love you!" He grinned at her, though, and she knew all was well.

"We are leaving in the morning," Alex announced. "Can everything be ready by then?"

Madelina looked at her mother, who nodded. "I was up most of the night, gathering the herbs and putting them into pouches. I have written out instructions on many of them. You will be ready."

Christiana smiled at Madelina. "And Eva and I spent the

night making new clothes for you and Letice. You will both be ready."

Letice looked at Madelina. "We leave?"

"Aye, we are going to go live with Alexander. His family lives three days from here."

Letice seemed confused. "You will not leave me?"

"No. I will not leave you. You will be with me for a very long time." Madelina hated that she was being taken from her new home so quickly, but it was necessary. Her mother did not need to raise another child, and it was her *only* chance for a daughter.

"You will not die?" Letice asked softly.

"No, I will not die. I am going to stay with you." Madelina felt tears drift down her cheeks, fighting against the rain she knew would come if she was not careful. She hated that her powers were activated by her emotions. She loved when she could decide what should happen, but when they happened automatically, they became a problem.

Throughout the day, she worked with her mother, getting the herbs put in pouches and seeds for her to grow more herbs in other pouches. They took a break for the mid-day meal and then got back to work. Many of the servants were working with her aunts to get dresses finished for both her and Letice. They were representing her family as they moved, and they would not look like paupers.

She had no idea where Alex was all day, but by his angry look at supper-time, she had a good idea he had spent the day with her father. She leaned close to him to whisper, "Is all well?"

He nodded. "Your father does not like me."

"He does not like that I married you. I think he likes *you* just fine."

"The results are the same." Alex sat down beside her, Letice on the other side of her. It still seemed strange to him that he had married her just the day before, and already they had a child. One part of him wanted the time alone, and he wanted to ask her to leave the child, but the other part of him realized that Madelina had a need to bring the girl with them. Whatever the reason for that need, he would not take Letice from her.

After supper, Madelina took Letice upstairs to put her to bed, and Alex went with her. The three of them sat in Madelina's childhood room and tried to explain what was happening to the child. "Because I married Alex, we are all going to travel together to the house where he grew up and that is where we are going to live."

"Alex is my new papa?"

"Aye, he is your new papa, and I am your new mama. Soon you will have lots of brothers, and we will all be a happy family." Madelina tucked the little girl under the covers and smoothed her hair away from her face. "Does that sound nice?"

Letice nodded. "I want to have family."

"You do have a family. I promise. You are mine now." Madelina leaned down and kissed the girl's cheek. "I will see you in the morning, and we will leave then."

Letice closed her eyes, her lashes long against her cheeks. Alex and Madelina stayed there for another minute while they waited to see if she was going to ask anything else, but when she did not, they tiptoed from the room.

When they had closed the door, Madelina looked at Alexander. "I want her to be happy."

"It will not take long for her to forget she ever had another family," he said softly. "She is very young."

"But we cannot let her forget," Madelina said. "I wish we knew what to tell her about her parents."

"Why do not you want her to forget?" Alex asked, confused.

"Because I want her to know that we chose to keep her with us. She was not a child of birth, but she is a child of our hearts." Madelina was not sure if she was explaining it well, but Alex seemed to understand.

"Whatever you wish where she is concerned," he said softly.

As they made their way down the stairs from the east wing and up them into the west wing, she yawned. "I had no idea how much work went into preparing to move. Mother and I worked all day on just the herbs and the seeds to grow more herbs. I hope there is a good place for my herb garden at your home." She was getting more and more excited about starting her life with him.

"I believe there is. Mother has a small garden each year, but it is usually flowers, not herbs."

"Will she mind if I plant herbs in it? I do not want to upset her."

He frowned at her. "My parents will move into the dower house after we get home. They will not live with us. She will have a flower garden there."

"Why not? It is their home!" She hated the idea of ousting his parents from their home.

"This is something they have known they would do since they came to England. They built a house on the land where they would live as soon as I married. I think they are excited to move into their new home. I know I am excited to be able to take over the castle and run it as my own."

"Do your brothers not mind that their younger brother is inheriting instead of them?"

He shrugged. "I never really thought about that. We always knew that I would inherit and growing up knowing that makes things different I think. It is strange compared with the way other families do things, but for us, it seems just right."

"As long as there will not be any angry wives trying to hurt me or Letice," she said with a grin.

"Oh, there will not. All of my brothers have children and have moved to other areas. They truly are content."

Madelina breathed a sigh. "Then I am sure we will be, too."

CHAPTER FIVE

As soon as they had broken their fast the following morning, Alexander announced it was time to load the wagons. Madelina had not realized just how much she had to take with her, but her uncle had announced that he would be sending four men with them, along with two wagons. That way they would be safer on their ride. His men would take turns driving the wagons while she and Alex rode beside them. Letice would ride in the wagons at times and with Alex and Madelina at times. The girl was not afraid of horses, and Madelina planned to start teaching her to ride as soon as they were at their new home.

Madelina embraced both of her parents, thanking them for loving her as they did. When her aunt Christiana embraced her, they came up with a plan. "Every hour or so, reach out to me with your mind. If I answer, you know that I will be able to hear your cries for help and pass along news from there. If I do not, you will know that you have to go back to the previous place."

"You really do not think you will be able to communicate with me from that distance, do you?"

Christiana shook her head sadly. "I am certain I will not. So, it will be up to you to find the closest place to your new home where we *can* communicate."

Thinking of how much Alexander hated her communicating with her aunt with him there, she realized she may have to hide what she was doing. It was a small thing, and she needed to have a way to contact her family. "We will make it work, Auntie."

Eva hugged her as well. "Stay strong," was all she said.

Madelina swung up onto her mount and faced forward, refusing to turn around and wave. As they passed over the hill that would hide the castle where she had grown up from her view, she thought to her aunt, "I love you!"

"Be safe!" came back loud and clear.

Madelina refused to cry because they did not need rain on their journey, so instead she kept her shoulders back and stifled her emotions. Alex watched her. "You are doing well."

She smiled, happy that she had fooled someone. She would never be able to fool herself, though. Half of her heart was staying with the people who loved her so much at the Nobilis Castle. "Does your home have a name?" she asked, trying to think of only what was ahead of her and not what she was leaving behind.

"It is called Lain Castle."

"Lain?" she asked softly.

"'Tis our family name." Alex could not help but worry about his new bride. She looked as if she was strong and doing well, but he knew how very much she loved her family. She would be sad for a time, and he would need to help her work through that sadness. "My father and mother are surely expecting us to return soon. I do not know if Father realizes that we are married, but it is a possibility. He often guesses correctly. It is part of his luck."

She smiled over at him. When one of her sisters had

married, she had hidden her powers from her husband, worried that he would not want her if he knew about it. She was glad that she and Alex could be completely open about their families with each other.

Letice spent much of the day riding with her new mother, enjoying being held as well as looking around her. She seemed content to sleep as they rode as long as her mother was still holding her.

When they stopped at the end of the day, Madelina's legs were wobbly, and her arms were half asleep from holding the child. They had put in a good eight hours on their horses, and that was the longest she had ever been on a horseback. Alex held Letice as she dismounted, his gaze on his bride. "Are you all right?"

Madelina nodded, laughing. "I thought the hours I had spent on horseback over the years would have prepared me for this journey. There is a great deal of difference between two hours on a horse and eight hours on a horse. I may have to limp off and rest for a bit."

He smiled at that. "I will see to supper tonight. I have eaten on the road before, and it is easy for me. There is a tent for us. I slept on the ground on the way here, but I did not think you would want to sleep in the open."

"Thank you for thinking of me."

"Thank your uncle. He sent the tent with instructions it be returned with his wagons. He did not want you to feel out of place."

She smiled at that. "Let me take Letice, and she and I will avail ourselves of the woods for our needs." She also wanted to talk to her aunt Christiana to let them know they had made it safely through the first day of her voyage, but she did not want to do it with Alex there. He had made his feelings clear already.

While she was taking care of her needs, she reached out

to her aunt. "Aunt Christiana? We have finished our first day of travel. I am sore!"

"Well, of course you are! Your mother packed a salve in your potion bag. Use it on your sore thighs. She promises it will help."

"Thank her for me and send my love to all!"

"You receive love back from every one of us. You know that without being told, though."

Madelina did know without being told she had the love of everyone she had left behind. This was the first night of her life she would not sleep under the roof of her uncle's castle. The first night she would not be protected by her father and uncles. Her life was changing quickly. She was not sure she was ready for the rate of it all.

When she and Letice returned to the wagons, Alex had a fire going and was working to put up a tent with the other men. He was stripped to the waist, his arm muscles bulging as he did his share of the work and more. Madelina had not thought before about the type of training he must do to keep fit, but apparently, he worked as hard at it as her father and uncles did.

"How can I help?" Madelina asked, wishing she could just get the salve to use and not have to deal with anyone.

"Rest until supper. You are not used to this type of work," Alex called back.

She started to protest, but she realized she really did need to rest. She went into her medicine bag and found the salve her mother had included, disappearing back into the woods to apply it. "Are you sore?" she asked Letice.

The little girl shook her head, her hair swinging about her face. Madelina knew she needed to start tying it back or it would always be in the way.

She was moving easier as soon as they left the woods and returned to the campsite, and she and Letice sat down several feet from the fire. She did not want the fire to go out when she called in the wind to keep herself cool.

The meal consisted of dried venison and some greens Madelina and Letice picked while they waited for Alex. "These are greens that will make us stronger," she said, passing a handful to him.

"You know how to find food from vegetation growing beside the road?" He was surprised but knew he should not be. Her upbringing had been very different than most young ladies.

She shrugged. "My mother has taught me much." She watched as Letice ate a bite of the greens and made a face. She did not stop eating, though, which pleased Madelina. The child had spent her life until now in poverty. She knew that if she did not eat what was put before her, she did not eat. Eventually she would learn differently, but for now, it worked out well. "The tent looks ready."

Alex nodded. "The men will take turns guarding the tent through the night. They can take turns sleeping in the wagons while the others drive, so they will be fine." He rightly saw on her face that she worried about the men guarding them.

"That sounds good. I have never slept in a tent."

He frowned at that. "Never?"

She shook her head. "I have never slept anywhere but the castle where I was born and raised. My family was not one for travel, and if someone did travel, most of the children stayed with whomever was left at the castle. Mother was frequently sent for when someone important was dying because she was known for her healing, but she never took me with her."

"That is probably because she knew you would be safer at home—and she was afraid you would make it snow on everyone around you."

59

Madelina nodded. "That is exactly why. I have been guarded my entire life. This is the most freedom I have ever known."

He eyed her curiously. "You are free, but you know you must listen to my instructions, do you not?" Most women knew they must be obedient to their husbands, but she had been raised so differently.

She shrugged. "I know that the man is head of his wife even as Christ is head of the church." She felt that there was much compromise in marriage, though, and she had seen that was just how it should be in the marriages she had observed from infancy.

"And you believe that?"

"I believe that there is compromise in a marriage. I know that there are times when our opinions will differ, but I hope you will always listen to my counsel. My experiences are very different than yours, and I may be able to provide insight into a matter you know nothing about," she said softly. She certainly hoped he would agree with her.

"But my word will be final, correct?"

She nodded. She believed that—mostly. In time he would come around to her way of thinking. She was sure of it. She decided to change the subject because she was not sure they were ready for their first big argument. "I cannot wait to arrive at your home. I am looking forward to teaching Letice to ride."

"With a saddle?" he asked, popping another piece of the venison into his mouth.

"I thought to teach her to ride the way I ride."

"It is not safe." He would not hear of her teaching any of their children to ride without a saddle.

"I am perfectly safe when I ride Buttercup."

"But our daughter would not be." He sighed. "I have a feeling you are going to be more opinionated about many things than I expected while we courted." He was proud to have a wife of such spirit, but hopefully she would also be able to bend to his will.

"I would gladly have shared my opinions with you then if you had but asked," she pointed out honestly.

"Mayhap you would have. I was too busy kissing you to worry about your opinions at the time."

She grinned at him. "Much to my father's dismay."

He shook his head at her. "I know you laugh about it now, but it was not funny at the time. He wanted to challenge me to a joust."

"A joust? Really? I have never seen one because I have never been anywhere. Do you joust, Alex?" She found she was fascinated by the idea.

His face softened into a grin. "I never have jousted, but I have been trained as a knight. There was just no need for me to ever try to prove myself on a mock battlefield."

"I would give you a token of my esteem before you rode into the arena. A scarf mayhap?" She was amused at the very idea of him jousting. Her father had held much the same opinion as he seemed to about jousting. If you were a good knight, you had no need to prove yourself on the grounds of a tournament.

He shook his head at her. "And what color would your token be, milady?"

"Oh, it must be the perfect shade of bluish gray to match your eyes." Madelina leaned toward him, resting her head on his shoulder. "Have I mentioned how fascinated I am by the color of your eyes?"

"Mayhap once or twice . . ." He found himself more fascinated by this creature he called his wife every day.

Madelina unexpectedly burst out laughing. "Look at the babe . . ."

He glanced at the child, who was now stretched out

between them, sound asleep. Shaking his head, he said, "As soon as we have finished our meal, I shall carry her into the tent. Are you as tired as our daughter is, wife?"

"Not quite, but I am looking forward to sleeping tonight. And I really look forward to arriving at our new home and sleeping in a real bed with a roof over my head." She looked over at the tent and frowned. "Not that you did not provide every luxury you could during our journey."

He kissed her forehead. "I will usually provide you with much better than this. But you will need to enjoy this as much as you can in the meantime."

"If it is too hot in the tent, may I make it snow?"

"Hot? Summer nights are cool." He sighed. "How about a cooling breeze? I prefer those to snow . . ."

"All right, but sometimes you take all the fun out of my powers . . ."

After he carried Letice into the tent, he left Madelina alone to prepare herself for bed. She carefully tucked the covers around her daughter, wanting her to stay warm and healthy; even though Madelina knew Letice would be plenty warm, she worried about the fever the child had had just days before.

She undressed and slid under a cover to wait for Alex. It was a perfectly cool evening, normal for July in England, and it felt good to her. She was ready for sleep.

When Alex entered the tent minutes later, he found his wife and daughter both sleeping peacefully, and he smiled. All was right with his world if his ladies were happy.

———

LATE ON THEIR THIRD DAY OF TRAVEL, MADELINA REACHED out mentally to her aunt. When there was no answer, she frowned. "How far from your home are we, Alex?" Her aunt's voice had sounded weaker and weaker in her head as the hours had passed. She had known she would be losing her soon, but until that moment, she had not believed she would lose her completely before they reached their home.

"Less than an hour. Are you too tired to go on?" he asked, frowning at her.

She was filthy, bedraggled, and exhausted, but she had the promise of a hot bath and a bed waiting for her, and there was nothing that would keep her from continuing their journey. "Of course not. I am ready." In fact, knowing they were so close made her pick up the pace. Surely, they could ride ahead and have the wagons follow them. She had her husband at her side and her child on her lap. What more could a woman ask for?

As they rode, she was vaguely aware of their surroundings. They passed the walled city of York and just rode a few minutes north of there. She would have liked being further from the city, but she would not complain. Home was within her grasp.

When Alex stopped in front of a large castle—not quite as large as the one she had grown up in, but very big nonetheless—she looked at him. "Home?" she asked softly.

He nodded, swinging down from his horse and holding his hands up for Letice. Madelina swung her sore body down from the back of her mount and moved to stand beside him. "Are your parents home?"

"My parents are *always* home. Now that my father has retired from fighting, he is content to stay at my mother's side. Mother says she wishes he would find himself a hobby that would keep him out from underfoot all the time, but so far, he hasn't done so."

She smiled at him. "When we are that age, will you bother me by being underfoot all the time? Or will you be a docile husband, obedient to my every wish?"

He threw back his head and laughed. "If you think there will ever be something docile about me, you are a very confused woman." He led her into the castle, calling out as they entered. "Mother! Father! I have come home with my bride!"

Both of his parents hurried in from a room off the great hall. "Introduce us, Alexander!" his mother told him. She frowned at the child in his arms.

"This is my wife, Madelina, and this is an orphaned child we found. We decided to keep her so Madelina could have a daughter." He smiled over at his wife. "Father, Madelina is the youngest daughter of Charles Nobilis, who is the younger brother of Roland."

Her new father-in-law stepped forward and grasped both of her hands in his. "I do not see any of the features of my old friend, but I am happy to welcome you to the family. I heard both Roland and Charles married well."

Madelina smiled in response. "They married sisters, and their friend, Hugh, married their third sister. All of us have lived in the same home. I was raised with brothers and sisters and cousins."

His mother stepped closer to Madelina. "It sounds like you have had a wonderful life. I cannot wait to start training you on running this old castle."

Madelina then broached the topic that had been bothering her for days. "Alex has said that you will move away now that we married. Please know that I would love to have you stay here with us. The castle is plenty large enough."

Lady Lain laughed loudly. "You think if I stay you will be able to pursue your own interests. It is not going to happen. This place is all yours to manage." She leaned over and kissed Madelina's cheek. "Welcome to the family." She reached out her hands for Letice, who was watching everything with interest, her thumb firmly in her mouth. "Come see your grandmama."

Letice looked at her for a moment before leaning forward and allowing her new grandmother to hold her. "Grandmama?"

"Aye, I am your grandmama." Lady Lain grinned at Madelina. "I like how you solved the problem with no daughters being born to the seventh son. Very creative of you."

Madelina grinned. "I thought so."

"I hope you will call me Mother, just like Alex does. Would you like to see your new home?"

"Aye, I would love that." Madelina lifted her hands to take her daughter from the older woman, but Letice just put her head on her new grandmama's shoulder.

The house was significantly smaller than the one she had been raised in. Of course, her uncle's castle was built with the knowledge that there would be three married couples living there with all of the children they bore between them, which ended up being seventeen. The house had *needed* to be large.

This home had been built with a different knowledge. The knowledge that every generation that lived in it would have seven sons. What an odd thing that was to know going into a marriage.

As she was shown the first floor of the home, including the kitchens and the storage rooms, Madelina could see the care that had gone into the home. "Alex is very excited to have Letice and me here under his roof."

"I am sure he is. It must have been strange for him being under your family's roof. Tell me, how long have you been married?"

"We were married four days ago. We spent two nights at my home, and then we began our journey here."

"You must be exhausted! Instead of the rest of the tour

before supper, let me take you to your room, and I will have the servants ready a bath for you."

Madelina wanted to kiss the woman's feet. "That would bring me a great deal of pleasure."

"I am certain. Being on the road is so tiresome." Lady Lain walked toward the stairs and opened a door at the top. "We will be moved out within the week, but for now, I think you will find Alex's boyhood room comfortable." She opened a door at the other end of the hall from hers. "We can put little Letice in the room beside yours that was his brother Philip's."

"Thank you." Madelina walked into the room and found everything perfectly set up. She sat on the edge of the bed. "This room will be perfect for now." She reached out her hands, and this time Letice came to her, getting down to look around the room.

"I will go request that bath."

Madelina liked the way that statement had been worded. She would "request" a bath rather than order it. It sounded like that was exactly the kind of family she needed to have married into. "Your room is next door," she said to Letice. "Would you like to go see it?"

Letice nodded. Madelina groaned softly as she got to her feet, walking to the next room. There was a firm bed and a nice window. "This will be just right for you. Papa and I will be right next door. All right?"

"Aye." Letice did not need a further invitation. She climbed into the bed and pulled the covers over her, shoes and all.

Madelina wished she could do the same, but she knew she could not be rude on her first night in her new home. She tucked the covers around her daughter and left the room.

CHAPTER SIX

After she had finished her bath, Madelina dressed in the clothes she had just removed. They were filthy, and she wished her other clothes were available to her, but they were still in one of the wagons. She used the salve on her thighs again, pleased with how well the medicine was easing her pain.

Descending the stairs, she was not certain what she would find, but when she walked into the room where Alex sat with his parents, all eyes went to her. "Letice is sleeping. I showed her to her room, and she climbed under the covers, shoes and all. I think she is as tired as I am."

"Supper will be in a few minutes," Alex told her. "You can get a good night's sleep after that."

Madelina nodded, sitting next to him on the window seat where he was relaxing. She needed his strength to make it through the night. She was so tired, she was not sure if she would make it through no matter what she did. "I would enjoy that."

He grinned up at her. "I was telling my parents about your family and the special powers the ladies have."

"Oh!" Madelina had not expected him to tell them about the powers, so she was a bit surprised. "Aye, the ladies of my family have very strange powers."

"I know that when Roland was told that he would be getting Sir Robert's eldest daughter, there was much laughter because she was reputed to be a witch," Sir Ralph said. "Is your mother a witch?"

Madelina was used to the question, and she immediately shook her head. "No, we are all Christians, and we wear the cross, which we could not do if we were witches. We believe our powers come from God, but we *do* have powers."

"But only the women in your family have powers?" he asked.

"Until this generation, there were no boys, so aye, the girls have the powers. I have brothers and male cousins because my mother and her sisters were able to fulfill the family's destiny by conquering evil." She knew many people would think what she said was nonsense, but with a family who believed in luck so strongly, surely, he would believe what she said.

"According to Alex, your power is to control the weather. Is that true?"

"Aye, it is." She was tired, but she closed her eyes, letting the snow fall into the sitting room. She opened her eyes when his mother gasped with alarm. Laughing softly, she ordered the snow to stop. "You will find that I cannot always control it, and there will sometimes be snow inside when you least expect it."

"That must make it hard when you are at court or traveling," his mother said.

"I have never been to court, and I have never traveled before this week. I imagine it will be very hard, but I will mostly stay home as I can. Our lands were isolated enough that few people ever visited, except peasants wanting to be healed." She had not thought about how much her family's isolation probably had to do with her and her lack of control over her powers.

"Who has the healing powers?" Sir Ralph asked.

"My mother, Marina. She has the power to heal with her touch, and she has been known to pull someone who had just died back from the other side. That is where Letice came in as well. She was lying by the side of the road, and Alex picked her up and brought her to me because one of the peasants told him I was a healer. And while I am, I can only heal with herbs and poultices. I called for my mother, and she saved the girl. Alex saw her parents' home being burned, so we decided we would keep her and raise her as our own. I want to teach her the ways of healing."

Both of Alex's parents looked at him. "Did you realize the babe was ill when you picked her up?" Sir Ralph asked.

Alex nodded. "She was burning up with fever."

"You have shown no signs of this illness?" his mother asked.

"None. I am a strong, healthy man, Mother." Alex grinned at Madelina, who smiled back.

"Would you be able to cure this disease if you were presented with it?" his mother asked.

Madelina shook her head. "It is possible I could if I saw it in the early stages, but most likely we would need to send for my mother with her healing touch."

His parents exchanged a look between them. "How would you send for her?" his father asked.

"My aunt has the ability to communicate through thoughts. She had a feeling we would be too far for her to hear my thoughts from here, so she had me try every hour along the way. About an hour south of here, I lost her voice in my head. If I have need of my mother, I can travel to that location and ask my aunt to send my mother. It would be much faster than sending for her by messenger."

Alex frowned at Madelina. "Why did you not tell me you were communicating with your aunt every hour?"

She shrugged. "I did not think it mattered," she fibbed. Truthfully, she knew it had mattered to him too much, so she had not mentioned it. She had need to be able to communicate with her family, and that would be the easiest way, whether he liked it or not. "My mother wants to be here when I have my first, so I promised to make sure that I could communicate with Aunt Christiana."

"Is that the aunt who married Roland?" Sir Ralph asked. At her nod, he continued. "There is not a more able knight I have seen. He was a good commander of his men and quite shrewd."

Alex wanted to discuss her communicating with her aunt more but decided that would be better left for when they were alone. "Madelina will have to tell you the story of how the three sisters bested Roland and his knights for a day before they took the manor where the ladies lived."

Sir Ralph smiled. "That sounds like a wonderful story and one I look forward to hearing."

After they had eaten their supper, Madelina asked where she could find her clothes. She wanted to be able to put on something clean the following morning instead of something covered in dust. She knew that Alex did not mind, but what must his mother think of her?

Alex was still down talking about the journey with his parents when she slipped under the covers. She was too tired to stay awake for another moment. Three days on the road, after two very emotional days at home, had left her drained in a way she had never been in her life. She prayed for her family and immediately drifted off to sleep.

———

WHEN ALEX GOT INTO HIS BEDCHAMBER, ALL HE COULD THINK about was talking to Madelina about her communicating with her aunt so frequently on their trip. He walked in, and she lay on her side, her breathing even. She looked very young in that moment, and he could not bear to wake her. The morrow was soon enough to make his displeasure known at her actions. They were married, and she should tell him everything.

He slipped into bed beside her and pulled her toward him, not wanting to sleep without at least holding her. It was amazing how just a few days of marriage had changed him. He could not wait until their sons started to be born, and he was able to mold them into the kind of men they needed to grow up to be.

———

MADELINA WOKE EARLY, DRESSING IMMEDIATELY IN HER hunting clothes. She wanted to make certain her aunt knew they had made it home safely. She realized as she went to the stables that she had inadvertently fibbed. The last time she had talked to her aunt in her mind was two hours south, not one hour. She would go to the spot where she had last tried to communicate and reach out to her every ten minutes after that.

She mounted Buttercup gingerly, still a bit sore from the long days of riding, but this time she would be able to ride at her own pace, racing across fields. Not having an escort as she rode made her feel truly free for the first time in her life. She did not stop to think about safety or whether or not Alex would mind her going off by herself. Instead, she rode like the wind, her hair streaming out behind her.

It took her half the time to reach the spot where she had not been able to reach her aunt, and again she tried with no response. Another ten minutes south was far enough, though, and her efforts were rewarded. "Aunt Christiana?"

"Madelina! When I did not hear from you again yestereve, I worried for you!"

"We are fine. I must ride forty minutes south of my new home to be able to reach you, but that does not feel like such a far distance. I am just glad we will not entirely lose touch."

"Your new home is good? Alex's parents treat you well?"

"Aye, they do. Alex does not like me communicating with you this way, though. He feels it is rude, and I am not sure why. I will have to make sure to do it at times he is distracted."

"Like creeping out of bed before he wakes?" Christiana asked in her mind. "That is not a good answer, Madelina."

"I know, Auntie, I know. I will do my best to get along with him and give him time to adjust, just like Aunt Eva suggested. Give everyone my love, and I will return to my new home now. I miss you all already."

"You are certainly missed here. Remember, your place is with your new husband, not sneaking off to talk to me. We love you!" Christiana felt sad in her thoughts, and Madelina was certain she understood. Her aunt was losing her, and if she was going to be obedient to her husband, she was losing their ability to communicate as well. It was a difficult situation.

On her way back, she rode just as swiftly, hoping that she would be back in the castle before anyone noticed she was missing. Her hopes were dashed as she rode into the castle grounds.

Alex was on his horse, heading toward her, pulling in the reins to stop as she stopped in front of him. "How is your aunt?" he asked, guessing correctly at her errand.

"She is fine, and my family is fine. They were worried about me when I could not communicate with them again last night. Now they will not worry again. They needed to know I was safe." She hoped she could make him understand that they were important to her, and she could not let them worry.

"I see. Do not you think you should have had an escort riding with you? You did not think you were unsafe out on a horse by yourself in the early morning hours?" He knew she was intelligent, but in that moment, he wanted to shake her for not using the mind God gave her. How could she ride off and not even tell anyone she was going?

"I always thought my family was being overprotective by making me leave with an escort." She moved her thumb to indicate the bow and arrows over her shoulder. "I was armed and ready to defend myself if needed. And do not forget, I do have the power to control the weather."

"You think that power could keep a man away if he wanted to hurt you?" Alex dismounted and took the reins of her horse, leading it to the stables. "I am very upset with you right now, Madelina. You put yourself at risk, and I will not stand for that."

"I am still my own person, Alex, whether I am married to you or not. I was careful, and I did not allow myself to be caught by anyone. If you need a demonstration of my power so you can see just how I can use it, I would be *happy* to show you." Her mother and aunts had spent hours and hours locked away as children working on learning to use their powers to the best of their abilities. That had never been necessary for Madelina because the fate of the world was not on her shoulders. She used them when she needed to, and when she accidentally used them, but there was no reason for her to *train* to use her powers.

He did not respond as he led the two horses into the

stable and then offered her a hand to help her down. She accepted, wondering exactly what was going through his mind. He was angry, there was no doubt about that, but what was his anger about? Was he angry that she had not taken an escort? Or because she had dared to speak to her family without his permission?

He held her hand and led her into the castle and up the stairs to their room. Once he had closed the door behind him, he crossed his arms over his chest. "That was a very foolhardy thing to do, and I will have your promise you will not do it again."

"Will not do what? Leave the castle grounds alone? Or talk to my aunt?" Madelina found she was just as angry as he was, and when thunder started rumbling there in the room, she worked hard to calm her emotions.

"You have every right to talk to your aunt. I am not trying to stop you from doing that."

"Good because I will not stop. I love my family, and I have the right to speak to them when I can." No matter how angry he was, she was not going to back down from this. He was not going to give up contact with his family, so why should she?

He shook his head. "You have the right to speak to them when I am available to ride with you. I do not want you going alone because it is not safe. You are obviously a gentle-woman, and you could be taken for the money your family will pay."

"I was safe. I just needed to tell my aunt that we arrived safely and tell her that I could not communicate with her from my new home. Why cannot you see I could not allow her to worry?"

"So, you let me worry instead? How do you think I felt when I woke up and you were not beside me? How do you think I felt when I then searched the castle and you were not here? What about when I found that your mount was missing?" He shook his head. "Your family may have been slightly worried when you did not communicate, but they knew it was a possibility. I did not know you would be foolish enough to leave my safe home in the early hours so you could let them know you were fine!" The last word was a shout, and instead of backing down, Madelina stood up to him and walked closer.

"I am an adult. I have the right to make decisions for myself. I am a skilled healer and a woman of power. I will not be forced to hide in this castle to be kept safe. I have done that my entire life, and it will not happen any longer!"

"You do not think that as my wife, you need to obey me when I tell you not to leave my property without an escort?" he asked, his eyes flaming with anger.

"As your wife, I think you know that I am a reasonably intelligent woman. You have to know that I am not going to do anything that will put my life in danger."

"But you already did! We are not close enough to Scotland for the raids to come here or for the fighting to be here, but the fighting is close enough that it is just not safe to be out on your own. Ever!"

"I will not cower inside this castle. One of the reasons I wanted to marry you was because you were impressed with my skills, and you understood that I needed to be free . . . I thought you did, at least. You are as bad as my father with trying to keep me locked up and calling it keeping me safe." Madelina could not believe her sweet suitor from days before had turned into an angry husband already.

"Were you not taught that a woman obeys her husband? Everyone knows that women cannot just do what they want because they are *weak*."

"I am not weak!" Her anger got away from her, and she used a blast of wind to knock him off his feet. "I am strong!"

Alex lay there on the floor for a moment, deciding then that he needed to leave before his anger got the better of him. Already he knew that he needed her to learn to be a wife and not just a woman who felt she had her own freedom. He did not want his mother to have to talk to her, but perhaps that was the answer. He knew his mother had always been obedient to his father.

He left the castle, going right back to the stables and having the lad there ready his horse. He knew he was acting strangely, but he needed time to think on what to do with his disobedient wife.

After he had left the room, Madelina threw herself on her bed and cried angry tears. She could not believe she had become so angry she had knocked her husband down with her powers. She needed to apologize to him, to let him know she would never hurt him intentionally, but he was already gone.

It was not long before she heard Letice crying in the room next to hers, so she got to her feet and checked on the girl. An unmarried maiden had time for crying and emotions. A married woman had to take care of her responsibilities. Especially if she was a mother.

She walked into the room and sat down on the bed beside the little girl. "Why are you crying?"

"I could not find you."

Madelina realized that the girl was still sad after the loss of her parents. She needed to be a better mother to her.

CHAPTER SEVEN

A lexander rode for a couple of hours before returning to the castle. He did not act as if anything had happened—at least not in front of his parents. Once Madelina had Letice down for her nap, she asked if she could speak with him.

He nodded, following her up to the room they were sharing. His parents had not noticed anything odd between them because they were in the process of getting all their personal belongings ready to move to the dower house. The furniture would stay in the castle, but all of their clothes and special items had to be moved. They had lived in the castle for more than thirty years, so the process was tedious.

Once they were in their room, Madelina looked at Alex with tears in her eyes. "I am so sorry I used my powers against you. I have no excuse. I wanted to show you I could defend myself against an attacker, but that was not the right way to do it. Can you forgive me?"

Alex sighed, wrapping his arms around her. "We were both very angry with each other this morning. If you need to talk to your aunt about something, I want you to tell me, and

I will take you to the location where you can reach her. I think that is a fair compromise."

She nodded. "I will let you know."

"Thank you." He kept his arms around her, his hands moving up and down her sides. They had not been able to make love since they had left her home, and he missed having the special time with his wife.

He scooped her up in his arms and laid her on the bed, ready to rectify their situation.

"Alex! It is still daytime."

He grinned. "At the moment, that is the furthest thing from my mind."

This time there was no need for an apology. Her pleasure was as great as his, and she understood why he had apologized before. She fell asleep in his arms, thankful they were back on good terms with each other. They had been married less than a week. They could not possibly already have a troubled marriage.

WHILE MADELINA SLEPT, ALEX WENT TO HIS FATHER, HOPING to find a good way to ask him about how to properly train a wife in obedience. He should never have married a lady who was so independent. Her independence made her hard to control.

"Father? May I have a word?" His parents were together, going through their things in their bedchamber. They would leave soon, and he wanted to take advantage of his father's greater experience before he left.

"Aye, of course." His father looked at his mother. "We will talk in the sitting room below stairs. I will be back up to help when I can."

His mother frowned. "You are just trying to get out of helping, Ralph. This is not women's work, you know."

"I know. I will be back soon!" His father closed the door and grinned at him. "Thanks for the rescue, son."

Alex shook his head. "Just tell her to have one of the servants help her."

"Are you joking? I need to be able to live with her for the rest of my life."

"I guess that is what I want to speak to you about. I need to know how to make my wife obedient. Is there something I can do to train her to follow my lead?"

His father sat down in a comfortable chair in the sitting room, and he laughed. He covered his face with his hands and calmed himself down, then he looked at his son, and he laughed some more. "Seriously?" he finally was able to choke out.

Alex frowned at his father, taking the seat across from him. "Obviously Mother is the model wife. She obeys you in everything. How did you train her to be that way?"

His father took calming breaths and wiped the tears from his eyes. "There is no training a wife to be obedient. If a woman is treated with the utmost respect and made to feel like you value her and her opinions, she is more likely to *want* to follow your lead, but you married a woman of power, son. She has the ability to change the weather. You cannot expect her to be someone who easily follows you."

"She rode out this morning, knowing I would want her to have an escort. She wanted to make sure her family did not worry about her because she could no longer communicate with them in her mind." Alex sighed. "I found her riding back to the stable, planning to hide the fact she had left."

His father nodded. "I know right now it all seems insurmountable, but I will tell you that you do not want a weak woman. If you married a woman who backed away from you every time you raised your voice, she would drive you crazy. Instead you have a strong, self-reliant woman. There is nothing wrong with that."

"But sometimes she needs to listen to me and worry about her safety."

"Mayhap she does. Mayhap she does not. What did she plan to do if something happened to her?"

Alex frowned. "She has a bow and arrow that she uses with great skill. She also has the ability to call up her powers, and she gave me a dose of those this morning when I confronted her about it all. She knocked me over with her wind, and I landed on my backside."

Ralph threw back his head and laughed. "Welcome to the world of marriage, son. She is not one who will be controlled. The only thing I can tell you is if you are a good, strong leader who makes it clear you value her more than anything else in your life, she will eventually be easier to make suggestions to, and she might follow those suggestions."

"Are you saying that instead of telling her not to go and talk to her aunt without me again, I should suggest that she might want to take me along next time?" Alex could not believe his own father was suggesting such gibberish.

His father shrugged. "Take my advice or leave it. You wanted someone more experienced than you." He got to his feet. "Now I am going to go back upstairs and help your mother pack up our bedchamber, so I can keep the peace in *my* marriage."

Alex watched his father leave the room, feeling more than a little surprise. His parents' marriage seemed perfect to him, and his mother always seemed to do what his father said. How could his father not have better advice for him than that?

He went out to the courtyard, where the men were training, and picked up a sword. He had a need to do some real fighting to get out some of his aggression. Making love with his wife had helped but not nearly enough.

———

Madelina was talking to the servants about what they planned to make for supper, trying to be the kind of good wife her husband was looking for, when she heard her name shouted from another part of the castle. She ran, following the voice. Alex was being helped into a chair, a great cut on his shoulder. "What did you do?" she asked, immediately tearing away his sleeve to get a good look at the injury.

"I was not paying enough attention during training, I guess." Alex felt like a fool admitting it, but his mind had been on her, not on his training.

"Let me get my herbs," she said softly. "I am going to clean this properly and stitch it closed. It is not going to be comfortable, but it will keep out infection."

He sighed. "All right. Get what you need."

She was back a moment later with her bag of herbs and a needle and thread. His mother was right behind her. "Will you go and get a bowl of water as hot as you can stand it from the kitchen please?" Madelina asked. She did not watch to see if his mother had done what she asked. Instead she took a glass of water she had been drinking from earlier and added a pinch of herbs to it. "Drink this down. It will help lessen the pain of what I am about to do."

Alex frowned at her, but he did as she told him. It was only a moment before he started to feel woozy. "What was in the glass?"

"Something to make you tired and feel less pain. You are going to need to sit back as I work on this." She saw her mother-in-law approaching with the bowl of water and a clean cloth. She immediately dipped the cloth into the water and began to carefully clean the wound. She knew from past experience that if she left even a tiny piece of dirt in the wound, it could become infected, and he could die from it.

She worked and made sure the wound was meticulously cleaned. Her mother-in-law stood beside her, wringing her hands together. "What else can I do?"

"Go check on Letice, would you?" Madelina asked.

"Aye, of course!"

Madelina was relatively sure the child would still be sleeping because she took long naps, but she needed her mother-in-law out of the way. She did not need to feel her son's pain as Madelina worked to heal him.

Thirty minutes later, she had the wound stitched closed. "You are going to have to spend the rest of the day in bed, I am afraid. Quite probably longer than that." She nodded to the two men who had helped him inside. "Can you get him up the stairs?"

She cleaned her mess up, and carefully put her herbs away, mentally thanking her mother for getting all of the herbs ready to travel with her. Then she climbed the stairs and walked into her room, sitting on the bed beside her husband, who was sleeping peacefully.

She wished she could get her mother to come and finish healing him, but unless an infection set in, she would not risk angering her new husband by riding to contact her aunt. She had been relying on her mother for many years to back her up with her healing, but now it was time for her to stand on her own two feet.

His mother knocked on the door, carrying Letice inside with her. "How is he?"

Madelina smiled. "I have cleaned the wound and given him some medicine for the pain that will also help him sleep.

As long as infection does not set in, he will be fine in a week or so."

"And if infection does set in?"

"We could lose him." Madelina had learned at her mother's knee that you should never lie to the family of an injured person. It was her job to set clear expectations, and she would not make things easier just because she could. Truth was always the best.

"Can you send for your mother to heal him properly?"

"I can, but I promised him I would not go south to contact my aunt without him with me. If I believed it was life or death for him, I would contact her without hesitation, but I think he is going to be fine without her."

"Would she have time to get here before he died if infection did set in?" his mother asked, the fear in her eyes heartwarming. Madelina could tell she truly loved her son.

"She likely could. I would do everything I knew to do to keep him alive until she arrived." Madelina smiled at her, putting her hand on her mother-in-law's arm. "I have done what I could do. There should not be any problems. I cleaned it well, and I will be very surprised if there is an infection."

"Thank you." Handing Letice to Madelina, her mother-in-law left the room. "I am going to the chapel to pray."

"That is the best course of action now." Madelina watched her go and then turned her attention to the child. "Did you have a good nap?"

Letice nodded. "I woke up, and I did not get scared."

"I am really glad. I am here for you now, remember?" Madelina was glad the child was adjusting so well to her new surroundings.

"I 'member. Papa sick?" Letice asked.

"He got cut with a sword during practice today, so I had to sew his shoulder closed. See?" Madelina carefully showed her daughter where the stitches were. "Someday, I am going to teach you to heal people as well."

"Like your mama?"

"Just like my mama taught me. Now I am your mama, so you get to learn." Madelina was thrilled the child understood what she was telling her. "Would you like to learn to make people better when they are sick or injured?"

"Aye. I do not want people to die anymore."

Madelina knew the child was thinking about her own parents, and she hugged her close. "People will always die, but they do not have to die too soon. Disease and injuries made them die sooner than they should."

"Papa die?" Letice asked.

"No, he is not going to die because I did what I needed to do to heal him." Madelina felt confident that he would be fine. She hoped the people around her felt confident in her, too.

———

THREE DAYS LATER, ALEX WAS FIGHTING HER CONSTANTLY. "I want to be able to train with my men. Staying in bed this long is ridiculous."

Madelina stood over him, her arms folded. "If you go out there now, you are going to ruin my good work and rip those stitches open, but I am willing to compromise. You may walk down to the sitting room downstairs and sit up and not lie down constantly." She could see on his face that he was ready to fight for the right to train, but she was not about to back down. In matters of healing, he needed to obey her.

"Fine." He did not like it, but he did not want to be unwell for any longer than necessary either. He allowed her to help him to his feet, and then she had to help him dress. "I feel like a babe."

She laughed. "You are not a babe. You are just injured, and I am not about to let you make it worse by being stubborn."

"Me stubborn?" he asked, shocked. "If I am stubborn, I learned how to be from my wife!"

She grinned at that. "As true as that may be, you are still injured, and I am still helping you. I want you to lean on me as we go down the stairs. There is no reason for you to try to do it on your own and fall."

He listened to her, doing his best not to put too much weight on her slender shoulders as they went down the stairs together. When they had reached the sitting room, he was out of breath and felt as if he had just run for miles. "I am so weak!"

"Aye, you are. You lost a lot of blood when you were first injured. You will feel weak for a while yet."

He groaned. "I want to be able to return to my training."

"I could make you ready to train in three days' time," she told him. She could tell she had his interest.

"How? I will do anything!"

"I could ride down to speak to my aunt and have her send my mother. She could heal you completely. I do not have that ability."

He frowned at her. "It is not worth it to me for you to risk yourself. No, I would rather heal slowly."

"It is the only thing I can offer." She was relatively certain he was out of danger and would not be getting an infection, but he might just lose his mind from boredom. "We could play a dice game?"

He grinned. "Do you know any?"

She shook her head. "No, but I would be happy to learn." She hurried to get the dice she had seen in a drawer, handing them to him upon her return.

Alex looked down at the dice and rolled them in his

hands. "There are many different dice games, but I will teach you a simple one."

"Because I am a woman and my mind is simple?"

"No, because you are going to lose no matter what game I teach you."

Madelina frowned at him. "Why will I lose?"

"I am the seventh son of a seventh son. My luck does not allow me to lose games of chance. For it to be a fair game, we would need to play something like chess." He was certain she had never played, but it would be good to teach her. It would take time and give them both something to do.

"Do you have a chess set?"

He nodded. "In the same room with the dice. There is a cabinet under the drawer, and if you open it, you will see the chess board and pieces."

She rushed from the room to fetch it, excited to play. When she came back, he quickly and expertly set up all the pieces. "This was the only game my brothers would play with me," he explained. "They all hated it when I beat them at every game of chance without even trying."

"I can see that." She sat down across from him and listened to his explanation on how to play. He explained things slowly and carefully as if he thought it would all be too much for her.

After he had explained about how each piece moved and about winning the game, it took her five moves to have him in checkmate. He stared down at the board, his eyes narrowed in shock. "What did you just do?"

"I beat you. Mayhap you should ask if someone has ever played a game before you work so hard to explain it in such simplistic terms." She sat back and grinned at him, pleased with herself for beating him so handily. "I think Letice is waking up. I need to go check on her."

He watched her go, a smile on his face. If there was

anything that truly impressed him about his wife, it was the fact that she was accomplished at so many things. It was also what scared him the most about her because her accomplishments made her feel powerful.

———

MADELINA TOOK ALEX'S STITCHES OUT AFTER A WEEK, BUT IT was a full two weeks before she allowed him to set foot on the training ground again. "If you feel even a twinge, you need to rest more. I do not want you being in a hurry to ruin the work I did healing you!"

He clearly did not care what she said as he hurried out to the practice yard, ready to work with his men.

Once he was gone, Madelina looked around for something to do. The servants saw to the cleaning and meals. They even helped with Letice. She needed something to do that would occupy her time. For a brief moment, she wished someone would hurt themselves so she could heal them, but then she realized just how selfish that was.

Finally, she decided to sit Letice down and work on teaching her to read. The girl was very bright, and there was no reason to wait. It would not be long before Madelina started having babies from what Alex's mother had told her, and she wanted her daughter to be reading competently as soon as she could.

Letice did not seem terribly interested in learning to read, but she truly enjoyed having Madelina's undivided attention, so she worked to learn. She practiced writing her letters and repeated the sounds the letters made after her mama.

It took two weeks of concerted effort, but by the end of the second week, she could read a simple sentence. Madelina had decided not to tell Alex what she was doing because it would be a surprise to him.

When he came in at the end of a long training session, Madelina invited him to the sitting room. "I want to show you something."

Alex grabbed her shoulders and kissed the side of her neck. "I would love to see anything you want to show me . . ."

She pulled away from him. "There are children about!" She did her best to quiet her quickening heart as she led him into the sitting room.

When he got into the sitting room, Letice was sitting there waiting for him with a big smile on her face. "I have seen her before," he whispered to Madelina, who sighed.

"Do you take anything seriously?"

"Not if I can help it, I do not!"

"Sit down beside Letice." Madelina waved to the spot on the window seat.

Letice took a page of words that Madelina had given her, and she pointed to each word, reading it aloud.

When she finished, Alex looked at Madelina with a shocked look on his face. "She learned fast."

"She did. She is a very smart girl."

"What am I going to do with two smart women in my life? I think it is time for us to start having sons, so I will not be outnumbered!"

Madelina laughed. "We will always be your favorites, though, will we not?"

CHAPTER EIGHT

Within two months of getting married, Madelina began losing her meals . . . all of her meals. She found it difficult to keep anything in her stomach at all. She knew she was expecting, but never had she seen morning sickness quite as bad as hers was, and she could not begin to understand why it was called morning sickness when she was sick every minute of the day and night.

After a full week of keeping nothing in her stomach, she began to worry that perhaps there was more involved with her illness than just expecting. She was using all the herbs her mother had suggested for a weak stomach during pregnancy, but none of them were working. Could she be expecting and have something else wrong with her?

She talked to Alex one night while they lay abed after Letice was asleep for the night. "I fear we will have to send for my mother. I cannot stop losing my meals. It is not good for the babe *or* for me. If we do not send for her soon, I might not be well enough to get to the point where I can contact my aunt."

He looked at her in alarm. "Are you that worried? Or do you just want to see your mother?"

At his question, she burst into tears. "How could you even ask me that? You see me not able to keep anything down. My face is white, and I feel like I am going to vomit every minute of every day? And you think I am only doing this to see my mother?" Did he not know her at all? She *hated* being sick!

He pulled her into his arms, running his hand over her back. "I am sorry. We will go there on the morrow and send for her."

Once Madelina started crying, she could not seem to stop. "I am sorry. I cannot stop the tears!"

He pulled the covers over their heads to shield them from the rain falling from the ceiling. "That is all right." His hand kept moving over her back, and when she fell asleep, the rain stopped. The covers on the bed were soaked, so he went to another room to get something to cover them with, shaking his head. It had been bad when she snowed while embarrassed. If she cried during her entire pregnancy, they would have a very wet home.

———

THEY LEFT LETICE WITH ONE OF THE SERVANTS THE NEXT morning, and Alex pulled Madelina onto his horse to ride in front of him. He was afraid to let her ride on her own in her weakened condition, but he was not sure he would be able to contact her aunt without her help.

She rested back against him, feeling frail in his arms. It was then he realized that she was not just trying to get her mother there. She was very ill. He rode carefully, the ride taking well over an hour, but he did not want to jostle her any more than absolutely necessary.

When they got to the point where she could contact her aunt, she bade him to stop. "Auntie?"

"Madelina? Are you all right? You sound weak."

"Send Mother to me. Please. I am expecting, but nothing will stay in my stomach. I fear I am going to lose the babe, and I might not make it myself. I am using the correct herbs, but they are not helping."

"Wait there and let me tell your parents what is happening."

Madelina sighed, resting back against Alex. "She is talking to Mother. I need you to make sure you can connect with her. If I cannot come with you, you may need to come on your own and contact her yourself."

His arms hugged her to him. He realized then that she was very worried about her condition. "Are you worried you will lose the baby?" he asked.

She nodded. "The baby and I may not survive. I have never seen anyone quite this ill while expecting. The herbs we give expectant mothers are not helping at all. There is something *wrong*."

His fear began then. She had not felt the need to go to her mother when he had been wounded because she had known she could heal him. Now she was sending for her mother. That meant something. "You are going to be all right."

"I hope so." She closed her eyes, trying to preserve her strength.

"Madelina? Your mother told me to let you know she is on her way. She and your father will leave by horseback immediately. She thinks they can make the journey in two days if they ride hard," her aunt Christiana told her.

"All right, Aunt Christiana. It was nice to hear from you."

"Hold on 'til your mother gets there. Do you hear me?"

"I will be fine, Auntie. Alex is with me. Would you reach out to him? I want to be sure he can contact you if necessary."

Madelina nestled against Alex, hoping he would take a minute talking to her aunt so she could just rest.

"It is very odd having someone speak to me in my mind," Alex said a minute later.

"She was able to find you then?"

"Aye. She said that if I concentrate on her face very hard from this spot, she will be able to hear me." He worried that he would not be able to do it, but he would definitely try.

"Usually only she can start a conversation that way. But because I have had so many discussions with her in my mind over the years, I can do it. I hope the same goes for you." She closed her eyes, ready to sleep as they headed back to the castle. She had no energy for anything else.

When they got back to the castle, he realized she was asleep and handed her down to his brother Philip, who had come for a visit. "Hold her until I am down, please."

"Is she all right?" Philip asked, staring into the pale face of a woman he had never seen before.

"She is ill. She is expecting, and she cannot keep anything in her stomach." Alex swung down from the horse, handing the reins to his stable lad before taking his wife from his brother.

"And you chose this moment to take her for a ride? You have never been the brightest of the seven of us, but I did not think you were stupid."

Alex sighed. "We rode out to where she could contact her aunt. Her mother is on her way. She is a skilled healer."

"Father told me she could heal with a touch. Is that true?" Philip asked.

Alex strode toward the castle, determined not to stand in the castle yard having a discussion while holding his sleeping wife in his arms. "I saw her heal a child who was on the verge of death."

He went to the sitting room and sat down, carefully

arranging Madelina on the window seat beside him. He had his arm around her to hold her in place. "Mayhap I should take her upstairs to sleep."

Madelina blinked, looking around her. Her last memory was of being on a horse and talking to her aunt. She saw a stranger in front of her and frowned. "Who are you?"

The man laughed. "I am your husband's brother. Philip."

"Where did you come from?" she asked, very confused. She looked at Alex. "Were we not just on a horse?" It was bad enough that she was weak and tired. When he moved her while she slept, it was unbearable.

Alex smiled. "We were on a horse. Your mother is on her way. My brother was here when we got back."

"I see." She did not, but that was only because her mind did not seem to want to focus on anything. "I am going to make myself an herbal tea. Mayhap that will help." She had tried it every day since she had begun to feel sick, but she would try it again. Something had to work for her, and she could not just sit around waiting for her mother to arrive. She tried to get up, only to be stopped by Alex.

"I will have one of the servants fetch it for you. Wait here."

"I need specific medicines from my bag to go into the boiling water."

"Then I will bring you your bag, and someone will bring you boiling water for you to add it. You will not get up." Alex got to his feet and hurried from the room.

"My brother cares about you a great deal," Philip said softly.

Madelina was not so certain. "I think he just likes knowing that the first of our seven is on the way."

Philip shook his head. "No, that is not it at all. I saw the concern on his face when he was watching you. That was not for the babe. That was for you."

"I certainly hope you are right because the healer in me

tells me we are in for a very difficult year." Madelina had a hard time believing she was going to have a difficult pregnancy. With all the births she had helped, it would seem she should have an easier time of it. She did not know why it seemed that way, but it did!

"You are a healer? I thought your mother was the healer."

"My mother has the gift of the healing touch, but she has taught me the use of herbs to make salves and healing medicines. I learned much from her."

"I see. You do not have the healing touch then? What is your power?" he asked, obviously fascinated by her family.

She smiled. "My power is a bit strange. I control the weather. Often when my emotions get away from me, it will rain or snow indoors."

"Really?" He had never heard of such a thing. "Can you show me?"

Now that it was September, she was not perpetually hot, so she did not want to have it snow on them. "How about a warm breeze?" she asked, closing her eyes and allowing the wind to sweep through the room.

"I like this!"

"When I am embarrassed, it snows inside. When I am ashamed, it hails. If I am sad, it will rain indoors. Living with me means you need to be prepared for any weather at any given time." Madelina rubbed her hands over her face. "And now you need to prepare for me to be ill at any given time."

"I actually came to see you because I was told your mother had the power to heal. I was hoping she would be willing to see to my son." Philip seemed hesitant to ask, but she could understand the need. If her child was ill, she would move heaven and earth to get help for him.

Madelina gratefully accepted her bag of medicine and a tankard of hot water from Alex. She found the right powders in her small pouches and added two different powders to the water. "What is wrong with your son?"

"He was born with a leg that does not work properly. He drags it everywhere."

"Mama will be here in two days. If you can bring him here, I am sure she will be happy to see if she can help him." She knew that her mother could help the boy, but she would not promise her mother would use her gift for another. It was not her place. She had never seen her mother refuse to heal someone, even if that person was bad, but she still would not promise.

"That would please my wife and me a great deal." Philip sighed. "When he was born injured, many said we should let him die, but I could not see doing that."

Madelina frowned. "No, of course you could not. How old is he?"

"He is ten, and he hates being different. I am afraid he is starting to be very unhappy. He worries that he will never be able to fight."

"At ten, that should be the last of his worries," she said with a smile. "I am sure something can be done. Please bring your wife with you when you bring him. I would love to meet her. How far from here do you live?"

"'Tis a two-hour journey on horseback. I will certainly bring her."

With Alex back beside her, she smiled at him. "Why did you not tell me of your nephew's affliction? Mother would be happy to help."

Alex shrugged. "Sometimes I think some are born with afflictions because they have need of learning a lesson that can only be taught by their difference from others. I was not sure if your mother should be brought in for that reason."

Madelina studied him for a moment, understanding his meaning. "I am sure if there is a lesson to be learned, your nephew has long since learned it." She peered into her medicine, touching a finger to it to see if it was cool enough to drink. It was not, so she set it down again.

Philip got to his feet. "I will go and get my wife and son and bring them to you two days hence."

Madelina nodded. "Mother and Father should be here by then."

"Father?" Alex groaned. "You did not tell me your father was coming."

"Did you expect Mother to travel across England on her own when you will not even allow me to go an hour away by myself?"

"I guess I was hoping someone else would bring her. Your uncle Roland or mayhap your uncle Hugh."

Philip smiled down at Madelina. "It was a pleasure meeting you, sister. I look forward to seeing you in two days."

"We will welcome you," Madelina said softly as she watched him leave. Once he was gone, she looked at Alex. "Which number brother is Philip?"

"He is the eldest, and his son Joseph is the one with the affliction. His oldest as well. All of his other children are girls, and his only son walks with a limp. I am sure it is difficult for him."

"I hope Mother can help. I have seen her work miracles with many different types of things. She has been known to regrow a hand that was cut off." Men tended to cherish sons over daughters, so she understood his brother's sadness over the problem.

Alex shook his head. "The powers your family possesses are amazing."

"They are. I have a feeling they will continue to get weaker through generations, now that the need for them is over, but perchance I am wrong. It would be nice to see some of my granddaughters have powers as well." She reached for the tankard and started slowly sipping her tonic. She prayed that it would work this time, and she would be able to eat and nourish her son.

Twenty minutes later, Alex was carrying her up the stairs. "Mayhap the medicine will help on the morrow."

She nodded, exhausted. If she could not eat, she could not be expected to help her baby grow.

———

WHEN MADELINA WOKE HOURS LATER, LETICE WAS SITTING AT the side of her bed. She was holding a doll that she had found somewhere, but Madelina had no idea where. She presumed Alex's mother had kept dolls in the house for her other grandchildren.

"Is that your baby?" Madelina asked.

Letice nodded. "She was in my tummy, like my brother is in your tummy."

Madelina smiled at that. "Did you know my mama will be here soon?"

"She made me not sick."

"Aye, she did. I am glad you remember her." Madelina had not been sure if Letice would be able to remember her parents at all. She was very young, and they had been gone for two months now.

"She is nice."

Madelina rolled to her side carefully, hoping it would not upset her stomach again. She had precious little inside her, and she could not afford to lose any more. "Did you have your supper?" she asked, unsure of what time of day it was. In her weakened state, she slept more than she was awake.

"No. Papa says we will eat when you wake up."

"Well, I seem to be awake."

97

Letice nodded. "Are you going to be better soon?"

"That is why my mama is coming. She is going to try to help me feel better." Madelina just needed to hold out until her mother arrived.

"Oh!" Letice seemed excited by that idea. "I know she can!" She obviously wanted her mama back, and Madelina understood perfectly.

"Well, let us see if I can get out of bed, and we will go down to supper with Papa."

"Wait!" Letice jumped to her feet. "I get Papa!" She ran from the room, and though she was not certain why, Madelina waited where she was.

A moment later, she was back with Alex. "I told her to come get me when you were ready to go below stairs. I do not think you should waste what little energy you have on the stairs." He scooped her off the bed, much to Letice's obvious delight. "And I do not trust you not to fall!"

"You cannot carry me everywhere for the next seven months," she protested.

"Hopefully your mother will be able to help. How long do you think they will stay?" he asked.

"You are worried about how long my father will be in your house, and the most honest answer I can give is, 'I do not know.' Mama will stay as long as she needs to for me to feel better. I do not think they will stay until the babe is born, but they might."

He groaned softly. "Your father will blame me for your illness." He dreaded coming face to face with her father again.

She laughed. "You did have something to do with me becoming this sick."

"Aye, but I did not know you would be this ill." He deposited her in a chair in the great hall and sat beside her.

"Cook made you a broth she is certain your stomach will not object to."

"I certainly hope Cook is right. It would be nice for my mother to arrive and for us to be able to tell her I am better." She seriously doubted the power of Cook's broth, though. Her mother's herbs had not worked, and if they did not work, nothing would.

"That would be my greatest wish—and not just because I do not want your father to be here."

She smiled at him, truly understanding his problem with her father. "Mayhap you will find something in common this time other than a mutual love for jousting."

"Make certain you have your scarf ready. It may come to that quickly."

Ten minutes later, they knew the broth Cook had worked so hard on had not worked for her, and she was back in her bed. "I pray your parents come on winged horses," he said softly. He was not sure she would live much longer without them. He had never seen someone become so ill from carrying a baby.

———

IT WAS LATE THE NEXT EVENING WHEN THERE WAS A POUNDING on the front door. When Alex rushed to open the door, he stood face to face with his wife's father, who still had a look of anger on his face. How could a man stay angry for two months? Would he ever come to grips with Alex being his new son?

"Come in. Where is your wife?"

Marina stepped around her husband with a frown. "He bade me to stay behind him in case this was not the right place." She looked around quickly, taking everything in. "Where is she?"

"Upstairs. We were not expecting you until the morrow." Even as he said the words, he said a silent prayer of thanksgiving. They were in time!

"We left immediately, taking no time to prepare," Charles said. "Our daughter is ill."

"She is very ill." Alex led them up the stairs and to the first room at the top. "She is sleeping, but feel free to wake her. She will be thrilled to see you both." He opened the door.

Marina put her hand on his arm, stopping him from waking her. "I can start healing her in her sleep, and it will be better for her." She walked over and sat on the side of the bed, her hand hovering over her daughter's stomach. "She is definitely expecting, and your son seems to be growing well. He is not ill. He is taking the nutrients from her, though." She looked back at Alex. "Christiana said she had been using the herbs we give to expectant mothers?"

"Aye, and they have not helped a bit from what I have seen. Cook made a special broth last night, and she could not even keep that down."

Marina nodded. "I have seen this before. Mayhap you can show Charles to the room we will have for the next few months."

"Months?" Alex gulped. He did not want her parents there for months, but if it meant Madelina's life, he would gladly allow it. He just hoped he had heard her wrong.

"I am afraid we will need to stay until the babe is born. I hope this is her only pregnancy that is this bad." With those words, she closed her eyes and put her hands over her daughter's stomach, concentrating as hard as she could.

Alex quietly left the room, taking Charles to the bedchamber he had used as a child, as far from his room with Madelina as possible. It was bad enough that the man was going to have to be a guest in his house for so long; he did not want to have to have a room next to him. "Will this room work for you and Marina?" he asked.

Charles nodded. "Aye, this will be fine. How long has Madelina been this ill?"

Alex saw a true concern for his daughter on Charles's face, and he realized that the man truly loved his daughter. "More than a week. At first, we thought she would be all right, but it just will not stop. She takes all the potions that she knows will help, and she drinks the broth made for her. But she is still not getting better."

"Is it possible she is sick as well as carrying the babe?"

Alex shrugged. "I do not know. She and your wife are healers. Surely one of them would have mentioned that if it were the case."

"True." Charles clapped Alex on the back. "Whatever it is, I am sure Marina can help her. We will be staying here for a long time, but at least our daughter will be well."

"Aye, that is what we really care about." Alex studied the man who had seemed to hate him. "Are you hungry? I can have Cook make something."

Charles nodded. "Marina was not letting me stop for regular meals. We made the trip much faster than we probably should have."

"All right. I will go have something made for you, and they can bring a tray up for Marina." Alex paused on his way out the door. "Thank you for coming to help her. I was afraid she would not make it."

"Now that Marina is here, she will be fine."

Alex descended the stairs, feeling that a huge weight had been lifted off his shoulders. His wife would be fine now that her mother was there. There was no doubt in his mind.

CHAPTER NINE

When Madelina woke the following morning, she was able to sit up more easily. Her stomach still rocked a bit, but it did not go beyond that. She looked over to see if Alex was still there, but instead saw her mother sleeping beside her. "Mama?"

Marina sat up, her hand immediately going to hover over her daughter's stomach, assessing her. "You were very ill. Much worse than you told your aunt about."

"I am sorry. I did my best to express how bad it was, but I was so weak and tired." Madelina shook her head. "I am feeling slightly better this morning."

"Good. I healed you while you slept. We are staying until the babe is born. There is no choice. You are going to need some healing every day. I think at first you will need some before every meal. This is much worse than I have ever seen." Marina reached over to hug her daughter. "Now lie flat and let me heal you. I want you to break the fast immediately."

Madelina reclined onto her back. "I would dearly love to be able to keep some food inside me."

Marina worked on her for a full ten minutes before

nodding. "I think you are ready to try something. We will start with broth."

"I think that is wise." Madelina rolled to her side and put her feet on the floor. "I have been so weak, Alex has been carrying me up and down the stairs."

"I think that should continue for at least another day or two. I am afraid you will become lightheaded from lack of food on the stairs and fall. That is my grandson you are carrying."

"Could you tell that it was a boy?"

Marina nodded. "Aye, it is definitely a boy. Not that anyone expected anything different." She got out of bed, still wearing the traveling dress she had ridden to the castle in. "I will go and fetch Alex to carry you down the stairs. Please do not attempt it on your own."

"I will not, Mama. I do not want this baby harmed any more than you do." After her mother had left the room, Madelina took a deep breath. She did not feel like she would be sick, but it was hard to tell. She did feel too weak to try to stand on her own.

Alex walked into the room a moment later, scooping her up in his arms. "Are you ready to break your fast?"

"Mother says I may only have broth."

"She told me that last night. I have informed Cook to always have some ready for you." He carried her down the stairs as if she weighed nothing. "I do think you weigh less than you did before you were expecting my child. I do not think it is supposed to work that way." Once he set her in a chair, he rubbed at the wound on his chest.

Madelina frowned. "Does carrying me pull at your injury?"

He shrugged. "Just a bit. It is mostly healed."

"Mother," she said to someone behind his back. "Alex was cut the day after we arrived here. He is still in some pain from the injury. Would you mind?" It was good to be able to call on her mother for these things again.

Marina shook her head. "Where?"

"It is nothing."

"Where?" Marina was obviously not going to back down. She came from a long line of strong women, and she was used to getting her way.

"My left shoulder," Alex finally said.

Marina hovered her hands over the shoulder and closed her eyes. "There. It was still not quite healed, but my daughter did a good job on it. You used the right herbs." She smiled at Madelina with pride. "You paid attention to all I taught you."

"Of course, I did!" Madelina thanked Cook for setting her broth in front of her. "I appreciate you going to extra effort for just me."

"Not just you, milady. You *and* the babe you carry." Cook hurried back out of the room. She was a woman of few words, and that was a long speech for her.

Madelina sniffed deeply of the broth, making sure the smell would not upset her stomach, before she took a spoonful. She did not notice when the others sat around her and began eating as well. When the bowl was empty, she pushed it away and patted her stomach. "I think it worked, Mama."

"For this meal. We are going to be healing your stomach before *every* meal, hoping that enough food will stay inside you that you can grow. Every bite taken and kept down will be rejoiced over. The baby is fine, but you are not. You look like you have lost all of your flesh. You are just bones now." Marina pushed her own plate away. "I want you to either spend the day in bed again or in the sitting room. Which would you prefer?"

"I am tired of being in bed. Can we go to the sitting room?"

"Absolutely." Marina nodded to Alex, who carried her to the sitting room. Once she was there, ensconced on the window seat, Marina sat across from her in a chair. "How do you like your home?" she asked. "It is not as big as ours."

"I do like it. Oh! And before I forget. Alex's oldest brother will be coming with his son soon. He wants you to heal him. He was born with one of his legs deformed."

Marina nodded. "I can do that. It is hard to believe I will be without my sisters for so long. When you feel well enough, you will have to take me to the spot where you can talk to Christiana, so I can let her know we are all right."

"The men could do that today, if you would like. Alex knows where it is now because he had to take me there."

"I would like that very much. Christiana and Eva will worry until they receive a report from us." Marina got up and hurried out of the room. When she came back a few minutes later, she had Letice with her. "They are heading out now."

"Oh good. I knew they would not mind. What is the news from home?"

As her mother filled her in on the happenings back at her uncle's home, she realized that she was no longer as homesick as she had been at first. She did not wake up every morning wanting to ride to where she could contact her aunt because she was content. She had her daughter, her husband, and she was carrying a son. All was right with her world.

"Roland and Christiana's eldest is finally moving back home. He found a bride in France and brought her home with him."

"Did he bring home the fortune he dreamed of?" Madelina asked. She knew that her cousin was set to inherit the castle, and he would continue on the family name.

"He did. He was very pleased with the amount he earned while he was hiring himself out. His little bride is sweet, but she does not speak English at all, so we are all speaking French all the time. I think Hugh secretly loves it."

"I am sure he does. Someone who will listen to him play his lute." Madelina looked up when someone stood in the doorway of the sitting room. "Philip, I was wondering if you would come today. This is my mother, Marina. Mama, this is Alex's brother, Philip."

Philip nodded to her mother. "It is nice to meet you. Did Madelina tell you why I was coming?"

"Aye, she did. I would love to meet your son."

He stepped aside and nodded to a small woman with sad eyes. "This is my wife, Sarah. Our son Joseph is coming as well."

Marina got to her feet, walking close to Sarah. "Are you all right?"

Sarah nodded. "I will be fine."

Unwilling to believe her, Marina hovered her hand over the woman's shoulder in a gesture Madelina recognized as her scanning Sarah's body for illness. "Are you having stomach pains?"

Sarah nodded, a tear escaping her eye. "For months, but the leeches did not help."

Marina wrinkled her nose. "I am not a fan of leeches. May I?"

"You wish to heal me? But my son is the one we brought for help."

"I can help you both. You are worth just as much as your son is." Marina had taught Madelina that many women did not believe they were worthy of being healed, thinking they were only good as vessels for babies.

Joseph walked into the room then, dragging his leg badly. Marina looked at him for a moment. "Are you in pain?"

Joseph shook his head. "No, I just cannot walk properly."

"Then would you sit with your aunt Madelina on the

window seat while I see to your mother?" Marina smiled at the boy, hoping he would know he would be helped soon, too. She had to help the person who was most in danger first.

Philip frowned at Marina. "Is she ill?"

Marina nodded. "She is very ill. I think something inside her is about to rupture, and it could cost her life. I would like to get it fixed before I move on to Joseph."

Philip hurried to his wife's side. "You have not said the pain continued. I thought the leeches fixed it."

"No, but I did not want to complain." Sarah smiled at her husband. "I was more worried about Joseph's leg."

"I am more worried about you living!" Philip nodded to Marina. "Please help her."

"Of course." Marina moved her hands to the woman's abdomen and closed her eyes. It took just a moment before she opened them again. "All fixed. If it starts again, have Madelina let me know. It only takes a moment."

Sarah smiled up at her husband. "The pain is gone! 'Tis truly a marvelous power she has!"

Marina smiled. "Now, let me get a good look at that leg, young man." She squatted on the floor in front of Joseph and put her hand on his leg, assessing the damage. "One of his bones has grown sideways. I can fix it, but it would be a painful process. Are you sure you want that?"

Joseph nodded. "I want to be able to run and play with my friends."

"I think this would be better done on a bed," Marina said softly. "This type of injury, because he is had it since birth, is harder to heal and a great deal more painful. He was made this way, so healing him is almost against the natural order of things. I can do it, but I worry about the pain it will cause him." She looked at Sarah and Philip. "Would the two of you be willing to come up and help?"

"What can we do to help?" Philip asked. He looked over at

his son, who looked excited and not like he was dreading the process at all.

"You can hold his hands and let him know you love him." Marina turned to her daughter. "You are to stay here. No moving. Do you understand me?"

Letice sat down beside her mama. "I will not let her go anywhere." She took her mother's hand and smiled.

"Good girl!"

Marina led the way up the stairs, finding an empty room. "How about this room?" she asked.

Philip shook his head. "I think he will do better in my boyhood bedchamber."

"You lead the way then," Marina said, obviously willing to do everything she could to make the boy more comfortable.

Thirty minutes later, the four of them traipsed back down the stairs and into the sitting room where Madelina waited. She looked at Joseph. "How is your leg?"

Joseph jumped up and down repeatedly. "It works!"

Madelina looked at her mother. "Are you all right, Mother?"

"I am fine, but I will need a quick nap before lunch." Madelina immediately understood that to mean before she could heal her again.

"Do you need help? Or are you really all right?" Madelina knew that before their powers had been enhanced, her mother and her sisters had often lapsed into twelve hours of sleep after a particularly difficult healing, waking and feeling as if they had slept much longer. They would have to eat great quantities of food to regain their abilities again.

"After a short nap, I will be just fine."

Madelina nodded. "I will wait here then."

Marina took her leave and left to climb the stairs to one of the rooms there.

Philip frowned at Madelina. "Does it hurt your mother to use her power?"

"It does not cause her physical pain, but it drains her. She has already done four healings today and the fourth was particularly difficult." She had heard Joseph yell with the pain, but he seemed so happy now. She was pleased her mother had taken the time to help the boy and his mother. "She will need to sleep for a short while before she can heal anyone again, and right now, she is healing me before each meal."

Sarah frowned. "We did not mean to hurt her!"

"You do not understand," Madelina said softly, trying to help them see what her mother was like. "Mother cannot abide seeing people in pain. Because Joseph was not in pain, she left whether or not he wanted to be healed up to him. You were in pain, so she wanted to fix you. She would not have it any other way."

"I see." Sarah shook her head. "We are going to stay with you and make sure you are all right until she wakes up. We saw your father and Alex leaving when we arrived. You do not need to be alone with just the servants while you are so ill."

"I actually am doing much better today. I kept down my meal this morning, and that is the first meal in weeks." Madelina put her arm around Letice, who was sitting as close to her as she could. "Have you met my daughter, Letice? Alex found her before he came to my home, and Mother healed her."

Joseph looked over at Letice. "I am your cousin."

Letice just looked at him with wide eyes.

"I have lots of sisters, too. How old are you?" he asked.

Letice frowned, but she held up three fingers.

"I have a sister who is three. I think you two will be good

friends." Joseph looked at his mother. "We should bring Avice over for Letice to play with."

Philip nodded. "We will do that soon. I do not want to impose on them right now while Madelina is expecting. She is pretty sick."

Madelina frowned. "I tell you what. Give it a month, and I am sure I will be able to walk around and do more things. Come then, and we will be thrilled to have you." A month was really much longer than she expected it to take her mother to get her back to herself. Part of the problem was that she needed nourishment to heal as well.

Sarah nodded. "We'd like that. I have four girls and Joseph. With Philip's family being what it is, I guess I thought I would have all sons, but only one so far."

"Do you want more children?" Madelina asked. She knew some women did not particularly want a houseful like she did. Not that it mattered how many she wanted. She was obviously having seven sons. No more and no less.

"I do. I would like to have another boy or two," Sarah said.

"Will you three please stay for the noon meal? I can have Cook make extra." Madelina wanted to get to know this new sister of hers.

Philip shook his head. "I think we have already imposed on you enough just by having your mother heal us."

"We really would not mind . . ."

"No, we will be on our way, but we will take you up on your offer of returning in a month. I think you and Sarah would be friends, and I would like for Avice and Letice to become close."

Madelina nodded. "That would make me very happy. I know she is looking forward to when her brothers are born so she will not be the only child."

Charles and Alex returned then. "Where is Marina?" Charles asked, obviously concerned.

"She did some healing this morning, and she wanted to rest before she had to heal me again at lunchtime. I think this is going to be a difficult time for her." Madelina hated to admit to her father that she had caused her mother to exhaust herself.

"She is not . . . ?" he asked, obviously concerned.

"Not at all. She said she would like to nap before lunch, and she climbed the stairs of her own power." Madelina immediately understood that he was worried she had worn herself out like she used to before her powers were enhanced shortly after they wed. The three sisters had always helped one another by boosting each other's powers when there was a big task ahead of them.

He nodded. "I think I will go check on her anyway. I want to be certain."

Madelina smiled and nodded. She understood completely. Her parents were linked in a way very few couples were because they had fought off the worst evil that had been seen in the world in their very early marriage.

Philip stood. "We are going to leave for our home. We will come back in a month as we said. Thank your mother again."

Alex looked over at Joseph. "How's the leg?"

Joseph stood up and walked to his uncle. "Look!" The boy was obviously very excited to have his leg fixed.

Alex squatted down to get a good look at the leg. His knee had been turned completely outward the last time he had seen him. "That is amazing. A true miracle." Alex looked at his brother and smiled. "I am happy for your whole family."

Philip led his small family out of the castle, and Alex sat down. "How are you feeling? Did you keep your food down?" He had been happy to talk to his brother and his nephew, but his real concern was his wife.

She nodded with a smile. "I did. Mama is going to heal me

a little bit before each meal, so that I can continue keeping food down."

"Sarah looked better than I have seen her in years. She must be doing something right."

"Mama healed her, too. There was something about to rupture inside her."

"No wonder she needed to sleep for a while. She worked on you this morning, too. She is going to be exhausted." Alex shook his head. "Should she do so much all at once?"

Madelina laughed. "Can you imagine trying to stop her? You think I am headstrong, but you have never fought with my mother about her powers. She would kill herself healing others if that is what it took."

"Well, at least I know you come by your defiance naturally."

"I come from a long line of women of power. How do you think women of power would take to being told to sit down and be quiet? I am afraid we are not known for our docile natures. Mother even tells stories of her mother, who was powerless, and she hid the three of them and had them work on their powers. Mama did not discover her power under she was six or so. The others had been practicing their powers since birth."

"So, she came into her powers late?" Alex asked with surprise. Marina was so adept at healing, it was hard to believe she had not done it from a very young age.

"You know, I am not sure. I think mayhap she just did not know she had the power, so she had never tried to use it. I only know that Aunt Christiana once cut her own hand so Mama could practice healing. After that, their mother made sure they were brought peasants to heal whenever possible."

"And their mother had no power? How was that?" he asked.

She shrugged. "I just know she was powerless, but their

grandmother had told their mother a story every night that she then told them. That story told what they needed to do with a man who sought to rule the world."

"I cannot imagine your mother fighting anyone or using violence."

Madelina smiled. "She could not. She healed his heart instead."

Alex stared at her for a moment, and then a slow smile spread across his lips. "A brilliant woman indeed."

CHAPTER TEN

It took a full two weeks before Madelina's mother thought Madelina was strong enough to go up and down the stairs on her own. It was another month after that before she lost the gaunt, underfed look. Throughout it all, her belly continued to grow.

A month before she was due, Madelina sat down with her mother and discussed whether she needed to stay longer. Madelina had finally stopped losing her meals and no longer needed to be healed before she could eat, but it had only stopped in the last week or so.

"I hate that you have already stayed so long," Madelina said. "It is nice to see Alex and Papa getting along so well, and Letice has grown very attached to both of you, but I think you could leave now if you wanted to return home. You are welcome here, of course, but I am thinking about how you feel."

"We are staying until the baby comes," Marina told her. "We have already been here for six months. What is one more? And I want to be sure you and the babe are all right before we journey back home."

"I love that you have worked with Letice on her riding. She is going to be the best big sister seven little boys ever had."

Marina smiled. "Aye, I do believe she is. Are you getting nervous about the birth?"

Madelina shook her head. "I am not. Now that I am not upset to my stomach, I am enjoying being pregnant. Well, I would like to not be quite so large, but I know that will happen eventually."

"Too many women die in childbirth for me to be willing to go home. I will be right beside you for this birth and all the others. I am not sure why you were afflicted so during your pregnancy, but I will not allow you to go through another minute of this alone."

"Are you going to move in with each of my pregnancies?" Madelina asked with a grin.

"If I need to, I will. I will not lose my daughter for anything." Marina reached out and squeezed Madelina's hand.

———

As she got closer and closer to her due date, Madelina realized she was happy. She had a sweet child, parents who loved her, and she loved her husband a great deal. He had never told her he loved her, and she had never said the words, but she was sure he knew how she felt.

She just wished she knew how he felt. He had never given her an inkling of his feelings other than talking to her about how excited he was about the birth of the babe. Being happy about getting a son and feeling love for his wife were two very different things in her opinion.

Every afternoon, they would walk around the area. Her mother felt that a woman who was soon to give birth—especially one who had been so inactive at the beginning of her pregnancy—needed to be very active leading up until she had the baby. She felt that women trained in much the same way knights did, but their battles were very different.

"I am glad you are getting along so well with my father now. At first, I thought the two of you would always hate each other," she said as they walked through the garden. It was early May, and the flowers were in bloom. Madelina and her mother had taken over just a corner of the flower garden for their medicinal herbs. The garden was huge, though, so it was still beautiful.

"We have come to an agreement. Because we both love you so much, and we know it is easier if we get along, we have made a real effort. Besides, he is excited to be a grandfather again, and he knows to see the grandchildren, he has to come through me."

Madelina looked at him in surprise. "Wait . . . you love me? Why have you never said so?"

He frowned at her. "Why do you think I was in such a hurry to marry you?"

"Because you wanted to bed me, of course."

"Well, that too," he said with a grin. "But I wanted to bed you because I loved you so much."

"I wish you would said something sooner . . ."

"I thought you knew! Why else would I let your parents stay here for six months straight? Why else would I allow you to bring home a child who was not either of ours? Why else would I dote on you every day and put up with your constant headstrong ways?"

She smiled, stopping there and turning to him. "I love you, too."

"I know."

"How?" she asked. She had thought her declaration would please him, and his simple, "I know" was a bit offensive.

"How do I know? Because you smile at me every day. You make sure you at least make an appearance of being obedient before you go off and do whatever you want." He shook his head. "I really thought when I married you that you would be obedient. I guess I lost my mind!"

"I am as obedient as I *can* be." She grinned, wrapping her arms around his neck. "I am glad you came to me with a letter from your father and a little girl who needed to be healed."

"So am I. And I am glad we have almost got your first pregnancy out of the way. Do you think your parents will feel the need to live here for all seven of them?"

She shrugged. "I think they just might. From what your mother told me, though, I should plan on having all seven boys within ten years. Then they can go back and live with Uncle Roland."

He groaned. "I thought they would just come for one week to make you better . . ."

She laughed. "I am still alive and so is the babe. Mother will not leave until she knows that is going to continue."

Leaning down, he kissed her softly. "I love you, wife. I love you so much."

"And I love you!"

———

THREE NIGHTS LATER IN THE MIDDLE OF THE NIGHT, MADELINA woke with a cramp in her side. She lay there for a while and realized that the cramp was coming and going . . . every few minutes.

She reached over and woke Alex. "You need to get my mother. We are going to have a baby." She felt the excitement and dread run through her in equal measures. With as difficult as her pregnancy had been, surely the birthing would be even harder.

He sat up straight, his eyes wild by the light of the moon streaming in through the only window in the room. "Baby?"

"Aye, baby! Now get my mama!" The man could move so fast when he wanted to, but now that she needed him to, he sat there dazed.

After all the trouble she had had with her pregnancy, she had expected a long and difficult labor, but truly it was short and easy. She was sure the easy was her mother's constant healing of her, and the short . . . well, mayhap the short was God's way of trying to make up for how difficult her early pregnancy had been.

It was six short hours later when Marina led Alex and Charles into the room to meet the babe in Madelina's arms. "This is Thomas," Madelina said, a smile bright on her face.

Alex sat carefully beside her on the bed, reaching down a finger to trace the baby's cheek. "Thomas."

They all stood and stared at him for a minute as if they expected him to do something miraculous, and then Madelina laughed. "It is not like he is going to jump up and run about the room! Give him time!"

That night, Alex and Madelina lay together in bed, and Alex pulled her close. "It is nice to hold only you again and not the huge lump that was my son."

"It is nice to only be me again. I was starting to think I would be the size of a house forever." It felt strange to not have her child living inside her any longer, but not so strange that she was not happy to breathe only for herself.

"You were still one of the smallest pregnant women I had ever seen." He sighed contentedly. "Do you think we can go through this *six* more times?"

"I really do not see that we have a choice!" She smiled at him. "The babe makes it all worth it, though, does he not?"

"He does. My firstborn son."

"I will be so relieved when it is our seventh born."

"Do you regret marrying into a family where you would be required to have seven sons?" he asked, concerned.

"Not at all. I am just glad I have my mother so she can keep me healthy as I give birth . . ." Madelina snuggled close to him, closing her eyes. "I love you, Alex."

"And I love you, Lina."

EPILOGUE

Madelina pulled the baby from her breast and laid him in the middle of her bed. Her seventh son, Robert, was her easiest child so far. He slept through the night. He was content to not be held. He waited while she dealt with his siblings when necessary. The child was practically perfect.

She set her gown to rights and walked across the room to pick up his blanket that had somehow ended up on a table instead of in bed with him. Somehow meant that Letice had brought him to her. She was the big sister they had known she would be. Already she was learning to be a good healer, and she was only thirteen.

Just as she bent down to pick up the blanket, it flew through the air to the baby and covered him up perfectly.

Madelina sat down on the edge of the bed, staring at the baby. "Did you do that?" They had once joked that mayhap the boys would get some of her power, but they had never actually expected it!

She pulled the blanket off of him, put it on the foot of the

121

bed, and looked at the baby again. Sure enough, he gave one little kick, and the blanket flew to cover him up.

She ran to the door. "Letice! Get your father! Now!" Then she returned to the baby and took his blanket away again.

Once again, he gave a little kick and grinned at her, the blanket landing on him just how he liked it. "You, my son, are going to surprise everyone. I had no idea you could do that!"

Robert just grinned at her, obviously proud of what he had done.

Alex threw open the door, looking at her. "Letice said something was wrong!"

Madelina shook her head. "No, not wrong, but close the door. I want you to see something." She felt a little thrill run through her as she thought about his reaction to what the baby would do.

He closed the door and stood next to her, looking down at the baby. "What do you want me to see? He looks just as he did an hour ago."

"He does. But an hour ago he was not doing this." She took the blanket off Robert and put it at the foot of the bed.

Robert did not hesitate. He kicked and gave a little smirk, and the blanket settled over him again.

Alex stared down at him for a moment, and then he sat down, too. "Did you do that?" he asked Madelina.

"You know I do not have that power. This is a power I have never seen!" She tugged the blanket to the foot of the bed once more, and this time the baby giggled as he kicked and the blanket fell onto him again.

"We joked that the seventh son might inherit powers like your family, but . . . I never thought it could happen." Alex shook his head. "Did you think it could happen?"

"I did not. I just hoped my granddaughters would have powers." She smiled at her husband. "At least we know he will never be cold."

"I hope he does not get hungry in the night and try to bring you to him!"

She laughed. "I do not know how that would go over . . ." She turned to him. "We must ride out and tell Aunt Christiana. The whole family will be so excited! There is never been a male with powers!"

"It is time then. Mayhap he will be able to get his wife to behave."

She giggled. "I certainly would not count on it!"

ABOUT THE AUTHOR

· kirstenandmorganna.com

SNEAK PEEK

ROBERT, THE MCCLAINS BOOK 2

ENGLAND, 1135ENGLAND, 1135

Matilda looked around her nervously. It was her first day of work at the Lain Castle. She had grown up in the shadow of the castle, and her parents were serfs who worked the land owned by the Lain family. She had been chosen to be the new maid at the castle, which would be hard work but would be much easier than working the land as her parents and their parents had done.

She walked toward the castle with her mother at her side.

"Ignore anything odd you see. The family is known for their strange ways. Just keep out of trouble, do what you are told, and you will be fine."

Matilda nodded, overwhelmed by the sight of the castle so close. She was used to seeing it off in the distance. She had lived in the shadow of the castle her entire life. "I will be home on Sunday," she said softly.

"Aye, you will. You were promised you would have every Sunday off, and you will spend them with your parents as you should." Her mother clutched her arm. "And if anything bad happens, you come right home to me."

Matilda looked at her mother. "Bad? The Lains are known for their love of the serfs. They are not bad people."

"That is true, but they do still have a son living at home. If you catch his eye, he might be interested in you doing more than emptying his chamber pot. Do not let him do more. You are a pretty girl, Mattie. I do not want to think about you being hurt."

Matilda nodded. "Aye, Mother." She leaned down and hugged her mother tightly. She was the only one of eight children who had survived to be old enough to work for someone. She knew her mother would worry if she could not see her every day. "I will be there early Sunday morning. Or if they will let me, I will come back Saturday night when my chores are finished." She hated the idea of her mother worrying about her, but their family needed the coins she would earn for working for the Lains.

"You are a good girl, Mattie. I hope this job blesses you beyond your wildest dreams." With those words, her mother turned away, leaving her to go to the big, bustling castle alone.

Matilda took a deep breath, squared her shoulders, and walked the short distance left to the castle. When she reached the moat, she walked across the bridge that put her in the castle's land. This was the area where the lord's army practiced for war and where the family would always be.

She kept walking and went to the back entrance, next to the kitchens. It was the servant's entrance, and she felt like an interloper. Pounding on the door, she waited, and a woman came to the door, looking down at her. "You the new maid?"

Matilda nodded. "Aye. I am to start today."

The older woman, who had gray hair and four black teeth, studied her for a moment. "You are too pretty to be an upstairs maid. We will put you in charge of dusting the furniture and sweeping the downstairs. It is about time Mary was promoted to be the upstairs maid anyway." She opened the door wider. "Come in! Come in! What are you waiting for?"

Matilda stepped over the threshold, forcing herself not to make the sign of the cross over her chest. The stories of this family made her very nervous. "I brought an extra dress with me," she said, holding up the bundle of clothes in her hand.

"Mary!" the woman called. "I need you to take this girl to her room. She is going to be moving into Agnes's old room."

Mary nodded and took Matilda by the arm, taking her up a steep staircase behind the kitchen. "This is where all the castle help stays, up here in this hallway. Agnes just married one of the local serfs, so she moved to his home. What's your name anyway?"

Matilda noted that Mary was only a couple of years older than she was, but she had obviously been working in the castle for a while. At eighteen, Matilda had never even dreamed that she would be living in a castle. She felt a bit like a fairy princess. "I am Matilda, but my family calls me Mattie. Have you worked here long?"

"Oh, aye. I have been here four years, and I know all the peculiarities of this family. You will learn them, too, but you cannot tell anything you see." Mary opened a door of a tiny room that had just enough space for a bed. There was a single window looking out over the courtyard where the soldiers trained.

Matilda looked around, her eyes wide. She had not ever imagined she would live in such luxury. "You mean I do not have to share?" Never in her life had she not shared a room with her parents. Their entire home could have fit in two rooms this size.

"Nah. Not here. The Lains take good care of those who work for them." Mary grinned. "Put your things away, and I will take you back down to Alice. She is the housekeeper, and she makes sure we all do what we are told and that the castle is always ready for guests."

"Do they have many guests?" Matilda asked, putting her extra dress into a chest at the foot of the bed. It was the only furniture in the room, but it was so much more than she had ever had before. She had been told servants usually slept in the great hall on rushes. Here . . . well, this was like living in a fantasy world.

"Not too many. Mainly just their grown sons coming back for visits with their families. There is only one son left here at the house, and that is Robert. He will be the one to inherit someday."

Matilda frowned, standing up to follow Mary back out of the room. "I thought Robert was the youngest son. Do not the oldest sons always inherit?" That was what she had always thought the nobility did. Had she been wrong?

"Not in this family. There is always something special about the seventh son, so he will be the one to inherit. I am not sure I quite understand it myself, but this place is different than any other in all of England. All of the world!"

As she followed to the bottom of the stairs and back to the kitchen, Matilda thought about Mary's words. The family was different. That could be good or bad. She just hoped it ended up being a good thing.

When she got to the bottom of the stairs, the woman Mary had called Alice was waiting for her. "For today, I want you to follow Mary around, and she will show you exactly what needs to be done."

Matilda nodded. "Aye."

Mary led the way out of the kitchen to the main floor of the house. "The work is simple and not too hard. You will need to dust and sweep and mop the downstairs every day. If there is something special Lady Lina wants, she will let you know, and you will do it. Very easy."

Mary handed Matilda a rag, and the two of them set to work dusting the main sitting room there on the first floor. Matilda could not help but notice what a nice space it was with solid oak furniture. She spotted a book and ran her hand over the cover. She had been taught to read by her local priest, who was something of a rebel. He believed women should be allowed to read the same as men were.

"You may read it if you would like," a soft voice said from the doorway.

Matilda jumped and shook her head. "Oh no, it would not be right!"

"I do not know why not." The woman who belonged to the voice stepped into the room. She had blond hair, and her smile was sweet. "I am Lady Lina. And you are?"

"Matilda, milady." Matilda looked down, afraid she would offend the lady of the castle by meeting her eyes.

"It is her first day," Mary said from across the room. "She is a little nervous."

Lady Lina shook her head. "No need to be nervous. I am sure you will do a wonderful job, and I would like for you to read the book. I could see by the look in your eyes that you wanted to."

"It does not bother you that I can read?" Matilda asked, surprised.

"Not at all. I read as well." It was a skill uncommon of women in the year of 1135, but the lady of the house was obviously not ashamed of being able to do it.

"You do?"

"Aye, my mother taught me when I was a young girl. In this castle, we encourage women to learn every skill they can, so they can be just as strong as men, though in different ways."

Matilda smiled, feeling as if a warmth had spread through her from her toes. "I would be proud to borrow it then, milady."

"Wonderful! Welcome to the family, Matilda." Lady Lina swept out of the room, obviously intent on making someone else happy.

Matilda turned and looked at Mary. "She is so nice. Surely she is not the mistress here."

"Oh, but she is. And she is the family member we will have the most contact with here in the castle. Lady Lina treats everyone as if she is a family member, and she even has skills with herbs and potions to heal people." Mary shrugged. "Many people are afraid of the family, but I promise you there is not a better family to be found in all of England. If she had thought you could not read and wanted to, why she would have taught you herself."

"Really? How does her lord feel about this?" Matilda was truly surprised to hear that a woman of the nobility was so kind to others.

"Really. He lets her do what she wishes for the most part. He is obviously a man who knows that women need to be able to exercise their own wills. Lord Alex is a wonderful man." Mary went back to dusting a chest in one corner of the room.

"I heard there was a son left at home, and he was well . . . odd." Matilda knew she should not bring it up, but she would be nervous until she understood exactly what she was dealing with.

"And how exactly am I odd?" a voice asked from the doorway.

Matilda closed her eyes, knowing this was the exact moment she would be sacked, and her good job would be gone. She would be back in the fields with her parents, toiling over land that may or may not produce a crop to the lord's satisfaction. "Excuse me?" If she played stupid, perhaps he would be lenient.

"You said the son left at home was odd. I am that son, and I would like to know just exactly how I am odd. I find myself very normal." Robert grinned at the new girl working for his parents. Aye, he was odd. Who else could make objects fly through the air at will?

"I am so sorry, milord. I did not see you there." Matilda waited for the ax to fall, wondering if it would be the proverbial ax or a real one. He was certainly in his rights to have her executed for saying something so rude.

"Apparently not." Robert shook his head. "Mayhap you should be more careful when you are talking about people . . . make sure they are not standing close by." Robert stepped into the room, fascinated by how pretty the girl was. Her skin looked so soft and perfect. He wanted to touch her.

"I will in future, sir." Matilda was not sure if she should curtsy or just throw herself on the floor at his feet, begging for his mercy.

"You know you will need to be punished for your bad behavior, do not you?" he asked.

Matilda heard Mary giggle behind her and wondered what had happened to the girl. Why would she be laughing at such a thing? She had thought they were building a friendship. "Aye, sir."

Robert smiled at her. "Now what should that punishment be?" He stroked his chin as if contemplating a great mystery. "Mayhap you should have to eat your noon meal with me."

Matilda blinked at him. "Eat my meal with you?" How was that a punishment?

"Aye, you have to accompany me for lunch. I think that is a fitting punishment. If you are going to be talking about me, you have every right to learn more about me, so you can speak truth." Robert winked at Mary, who was still laughing. "I will come to find you just before the meal. Be ready to sit with the family." With those words, he was gone, stopping just out of view and sitting down.

"Robert?" his mother asked from behind him. "Is something wrong?"

Robert shook his head, laughing. "Not in the way you mean, Mother."

"Then what is it? Why are you not outside training with your men?"

"Would you believe I just met the woman I am going to marry?" he asked.

She grinned at him. "The new maid? She reads, you know." Her face told him how much she approved of his choice.

"I am not surprised. She is eating lunch with the family today as my guest." Robert got to his feet. "It is too bad Grandmother is not here. Her powers may be able to calm my rapidly beating heart."

His mother stood on tiptoe and kissed his cheek. "You do not have a need of being healed, son. Falling in love is one of the most natural things in the whole world." She patted his arm. "Now go and train. You should speak to your father."

He frowned for a moment. "Is not this the day we were to ride so you could let Aunt Christiana know all is well and get the news from home?" He had never met his aunt, but he had heard stories of her his entire life. His grandmother had visited for a month at least once a year, but his aunts had not. He knew his aunt Christiana, his grandmother's sister, had the power to speak to people in their minds. His aunt Eva, his grandmother's other sister, had the power to make illusions appear before people they believed were real.

She frowned at him. "It is the day we are supposed to

ride. Let me take your father with me today instead. We will pack a picnic lunch."

He grinned. "Trying to leave me alone with the new maid, Mother?"

"Me? I have never been known as a matchmaker."

"Not to anyone but your children." He leaned down and hugged her. "Stay safe on your journey and thank you for the opportunity to be alone with her. I just wish I knew her name . . ."

"Matilda. Her name is Matilda, and she has my permission to borrow any book that interests her." His mother strode out of the castle then, and he knew she was off to tell his father she wanted him to ride with her to speak to her aunt.

Robert was left alone in the great hall of the castle, a smile upon his face.

————

Matilda looked over at Mary, her eyes still wide. "Why did you not help me? You just stood there laughing!"

Mary grinned. "Because I know this family. When he said he would have to punish you, I could do nothing but laugh. I knew that was not what would happen. Robert is a good man."

"But . . . he said he is punishing me by making me eat the noon meal with him. What will he do?" Matilda had heard stories about lords who took advantage of their female staff.

"He will have a meal with you, and you will get to eat the meal meant for the family, not for the staff. I am sure it will be a lovely, enjoyable meal, and you will get to know the people who employ us. I wish I was invited!" Mary grinned at her, getting back to her work. "There is nothing to worry about. His parents will be right there."

"But . . . the stories about him . . ."

"Aye, he is odd. He treats servants as equals. I have never seen anything odder than that, have you?"

Matilda did not respond, her mind on the face of the man whom she had met a short while before. Her mother had warned her against falling for one of the members of the family she worked for, but how could she help it? He had a strong, handsome face, and he had shown her attention. She closed her eyes, saying a prayer that she would be able to hold out until she went home on Sunday. Falling at the feel of her employer's youngest son would not be the way to keep her job.

———

Robert had a hard time paying attention to his training that morning. With his father gone, he was leading the different exercises, but his mind was not on training at all. Nay, it was on the pretty new maid. He wanted to ask her a million questions, and he did not want to have to wait until the noon meal to do it.

Never had he met a woman who looked so right to him. He knew his parents did not care if he married a noble-woman or a peasant. His own sister had been adopted from peasant parents long before he was born. She had always been treated as if she had been born a noblewoman.

When it was finally time for the meal, he called a halt to the training. "You may have a longer meal break than usual," he called out. "Twice as long would be perfect!" He did not stand around listening to his men cheer. Instead he went into the castle to find the pretty maid. Matilda. Even her name rolled off his tongue. She was going to be his, and he did not even care what she had to say about it.

He found her a moment later in a smaller sitting room,

polishing the furniture. "It is time for your punishment, Matilda." Robert kept his voice stern, but he could not keep the smile from his face.

Matilda turned to him with a smile, trying to act like the meal she was to share with him did not frighten her at all. "I am ready, milord."

He offered her his arm, and she was startled at first, but she took it, walking with him to the great hall for their meal. "Tell me about yourself, Matilda. How long have you worked here?"

"Today is my first day. It is a beautiful place to work."

"And a beautiful place to live. Have you moved into the castle?" He arrived at the big table in the great hall and made sure he sat beside her.

"Where are you parents?" she asked, startled.

"They went to talk to my aunt. Have you moved into the castle?" He repeated his question, determined to learn everything he could about her.

"Aye, I took the room of Agnes, who married recently." Matilda was relatively certain he would have no idea anyone named Agnes had ever worked there, but she told him whose room she had anyway. Mayhap someone would know.

"Ah! I was at her wedding on Saturday. There was much dancing and merriment."

"You attended the wedding of a servant?" Her eyes were wide as she questioned him.

"Aye, I did. In our household, we treat servants as members of the family."

She studied him for a moment as Alice served them their meal. She had put their food all into one trencher, and she smiled at Matilda, letting her know that the other staff did not mind where she was eating. "That is very odd, milord."

"Aye, it is when you think about how most things are done, but my family tends to have secrets they do not want others to know about. By treating our servants as family, we have their loyalty, and they do not tell our family's secrets." He reached out and cut off a piece of the chicken in the trencher.

"And what are those secrets?" she asked. She could not stop herself if she wanted to. All her life she had heard whispers about the secrets of the family in the castle, but no one had known exactly what those secrets were!

"Are you ready for our secrets?" he asked her softly. "Are you ready to swear undying loyalty and keep the secret until your death, if that is required of you?"

She swallowed hard, almost afraid of what the big secret would entail. "Aye, milord. I am ready."

"My mother has the ability to control the weather. I have seen it rain, snow, and blow wind indoors more times than I can count."

She blinked at him for a moment before laughing. "it is not possible!"

He went on as if she had not interrupted. "And I have the ability to move things with my mind."

She shook her head, a huge smile on her face. "Oh, but you are funny."

"May I?" he asked.

Matilda grinned, waiting for him to do something. She knew it was impossible. If someone could do such a thing, why they would have to be a witch, and they would not be tolerated by the church. He and his family were in good standing with the church. "Aye, please."

Robert did not have to look at her to see her laughter. She did not believe him, and he understood that. Not many would. His family was odd. His father was the seventh son of a seventh son, going as far back as the family knew. Definitely back into their Viking history. When his father had married his mother—a woman descended from a long line of druids, his father's luck as the seventh son had combined with his mother's druid heritage . . . and he was born with the power to move objects with his mind. It was odd, and he was the first to admit it.

He looked straight ahead as he picked up a chair from the other side of the table, lifting it onto the end of the table and setting it down.

Matilda gasped. "How did you do that?"

"I just told you. I have the ability to move things with my mind. I know it sounds like a story for children, but it is not. it is true in my case."

Made in the
USA
Columbia, SC